Praise for *The Best Small Fictions* Series

"Each story is a mini-masterwork, poised not only to entertain and enchant but to potentially serve to instruct the apprentice in the art of creating excellent flash."

— *C.T. D'Alessandro*

"This year's edition of BSF [2017] is a clear indication that the series is nowhere near a slowing down point, but is instead gaining momentum and prestige throughout the world of literature."

— *Enclave/CCM-Entropy*

"It will be well worth your while to spend a minute or 60 with some of the brightest concise writing available today."

— *NewPages*

"The best of these fictional vignettes are like a splash of ice water in the face. Wake up, they shout, your life is unspooling. They create their emotional effects with a quick windup and a powerful release, often a final, lingering image."

— *Harvard Review*

"In this extraordinary collection of small fictions ... readers are gifted with stories that slap wings onto their backs or drop anchors into their hearts, oftentimes both."

— *The Small Press Review*

The Best Small Fictions 2018

The Best Small Fictions
2018

Guest Editor
Aimee Bender

Series Editor
Sherrie Flick

BRADDOCK AVENUE BOOKS
UNCOMMON BOOKS · UNCOMMON READERS

For Braddock Avenue Books

Editors and Advisory Board
Guest Editor: Aimee Bender
Series Editor: Sherrie Flick
Chauna Craig, Assistant Editor, Domestic
Michelle Elvy, Assistant Editor, International

Consulting Editors
Dinty Moore
Christopher Allen
Michelle Ross
Stefanie Freele
Mauricio Kilwein Guevara

General Advisory Board
Michael Cocchiarale
Kathy Fish
X. J. Kennedy
Pamela Painter
Robert Shapard
Mary M. Slechta
James Thomas
Clare MacQueen

Founding Series Editor
Tara Lynn Masih

Printed in the United States of America
10 9 8 7 6 5 4 3 2 1

FIRST EDITION, September 2018

ISBN 10: 0-9989667-7-9
ISBN 13: 978-0-9989667-7-9

Cover design by Karen Antonelli
Interior design by Savannah Adams

Braddock Avenue Books
P.O. Box 502
Braddock, PA 15104

www.braddockavenuebooks.com

Braddock Avenue Books is distributed by Small Press Distribution.

For Zach Doss
(1984-2018)

Contents

Foreword

After hitting the ground running, taking the hand-off from the ultra-capable Tara Masih, who is founder and served as series editor for BSF for three years, I got up some speed and jumped, arms splayed, into volume four. What a tremendously rewarding experience it has been. Now I'm handing the red pencil baton to writer and editor, Nathan Leslie, who will dive into creating *The Best Small Fictions 2019*.

As with most collected book projects, a larger narrative began to rise from the nominations. A kind of big-picture story of 2017. Something about babies (alive and dead and gestating), wolves, birds, pigs, and blow jobs. Something about the cracked and forming fissures in the United States and other countries. Something that felt on the brink of something else, much bigger than any of us. Assistant editor Chauna Craig and I spent an evening with a bottle of wine and this book's pages spread on my kitchen table. We made stacks of very sad, not as sad, and sort of happy stories. We made margin notes identifying repeated concepts and objects. We knew we wanted the anthology to start with "Collective Nouns" and end with "Cassandra." We wanted to bring you up and down and down again and up. The order came together in eight "movements" as we started to call them. These movements aren't visible to the reader but serve as the scaffolding to an anthology that can be read as a collective whole or as random, individual 1000-word-or-less stories. An anthology filled with singular, unique voices and ideas.

I must confess: I'm in love with this book.

An anthology takes a village to bring it to print. I have so many people to thank and spotlight. First, my rock-star band of roving editors: Jolene McIlwain, Beth Gilstrap-Barnes, Aubrey Hirsch, and Ron Maclean. Their dedication to mining the tiniest journal in print and online contributed immensely to the diversity and strength of the nominations. I'd also like to thank my consulting editors who stepped in to help in key moments of indecision: Dinty Moore, Mauricio Kilwein Guevara, Christopher Allen, Michelle Ross, and Stefanie Freele. Thank you also to our advisory board, especially Mary Slechta.

This edition simply wouldn't exist without assistant editors Chauna Craig (domestic) and Michelle Elvy (international), who worked countless hours reading nominations, keeping our social media accounts lively, proofing, managing interns, and everything else in between. Speaking of interns, we had two outstanding young women helping us: Rebecca Larch (IUP) and Madison Brown (UALR). Thank you for all of your hard work. I'd like to thank everyone at Braddock Avenue Books for being great friends and patient editors, cover designers, website content updaters, and interior content designers—Jeffrey Condran, Robert Peluso, Karen Antonelli, and Savannah Adams.

I also want to thank all of the editors out there in the world who took the time to send in nominations. We appreciate your support. You are doing a tremendous and often thankless job! And, of course, all the writers who have taken such care with the language of their short fiction. It was stunning and an honor to read and reread your work.

Finally, I'd like to thank our fantastic guest editor, Aimee Bender. She was as wonderful to work with as her stories are to read. And she had a tough job this year. We had 101 finalists and 15 semifinalists. She took those 101 finalists down to 53 winners. She called her reading experience "exhilarating, liberating."

I can't walk away from thanking people without including my husband, Rick Schweikert. He does so much to make my life better each day, including making me stovetop espresso every single morning.

I hope you enjoy reading this anthology as much as we enjoyed creating it. I hope you emerge from its pages a changed person.

–Sherrie Flick

Introduction

I've judged quite a few fiction contests before, so it was a surprise to me how different this one felt. Once I received the packet in the mail, I sat down on my bed with the hefty stack and at first, before I read a page, felt a wave of overwhelm—how would I pick? How many actually were in here? I turned the page and began "Collective Nouns," a piece I'd actually encountered in the wilds of the Internet before this contest and had loved, and my readership suddenly started to crack open with possibility. But it was not just running into a story I'd met before, had loved before; it was the experience you are about to have, of living in one world for a moment, and then turning the page to enter another fully-realized one just after. It was exhilarating—sitting there on my bed, I could feel myself getting energized. I'd jump into one story, immerse myself in that writer's voice and vision and then switch to the next, get swept away again. It was actually very hard to eliminate anyone. Each piece made a kind of case for itself—with little bits of magic, moments captured in time, experimentation on the page, thoughtful realism, all of it, and I found it entirely rejuvenating to be reminded of the largeness that can happen in such a small space.

Here are armadillos that somehow embody feeling, a woman transformed, possibly, into something highly unexpected, old friends having a potent moment on a bus, surfers and fruit, a wild and precise Cassandra, walking infants, aggressive chewing, the complications of siblings and doll-houses, a date at a bar that reveals the complexity of love, unusual lists, the actions of pigs, wolves, loss in so many shapes and sizes, the ring of truth in a line like "the time traveler will always land in the volcano," and the curious question about why that phrase is moving, why, oh why? It can't be explained. It just rings right.

When picking, it came down really mainly to this. To a right kind of ringing. To the words below the words. Or, not the words—the sensation, the experience floating up through the words that uses the words to convey something underneath. I don't care about what a writer chooses to write about, but I want to feel the words doing their thing on the page without too much writerly interference. And all of these do that, beautifully—they are weird, they are straight-forward, they are luscious or spare, but they are all guided by a push underneath the language that then comes across to the reader as a movement, a flow.

While I was reading through these stories, over a series of many days, I received some very sad news, which was that one of my graduate students in fiction at USC had died unex-pectedly. His name was Zach Doss, and he was a wonderful writer of flash fiction, and a great reader and supporter of it, too. You can find his very fine work online. He would've loved these stories, and it feels right to dedicate the book to him, a true aficionado of the short-short, from all sides of the page.

I commend all these writers, and I look forward to my own copy of this anthology, to seeing them all side by side, this leaping from one active mind to the next.

–Aimee Bender

The Best Small Fictions 2018

Kathy Fish :
Collective Nouns for Humans in the Wild

[From *Jellyfish Review*, Issue 24, Sept.-Oct. 2017]

A group of grandmothers is a *tapestry*. A group of toddlers, a *jubilance* (see also: a *bewailing*). A group of librarians is an *enlightenment*. A group of visual artists is a *bioluminescence*. A group of short story writers is a *Flannery*. A group of musicians is — a *band*.

A *resplendence* of poets.
A *beacon* of scientists.
A *raft* of social workers.

A group of first responders is a *valiance*. A group of peaceful protestors is a *dream*. A group of special education teachers is a *transcendence*. A group of neonatal ICU nurses is a *divinity*. A group of hospice workers, a *grace*.

Humans in the wild, gathered and feeling good, previously an *exhilaration*, now: a *target*.

1

Kathy Fish

A *target* of concert-goers.
A *target* of movie-goers.
A *target* of dancers.

A group of schoolchildren is a *target*.

Kathy Fish teaches for the Mile High MFA at Regis University in Denver, Colorado. Her flash fiction, short stories, and prose poems have been widely published and anthologized. She has published four collections of short fiction: a chapbook in the Rose Metal Press collective, *A Peculiar Feeling of Restlessness: Four Chapbooks of Short Short Fiction by Four Women* (2008), *Wild Life* (Matter Press, 2011), *Together We Can Bury It* (The Lit Pub, 2012), and *Rift*, co-authored with Robert Vaughan (Unknown Press, 2015). Her work has been previously selected for *The Best Small Fictions* by Stuart Dybek and Amy Hempel.

Bud Smith :
Wolves

[From *SmokeLong Quarterly*, Issue Fifty-Five, February 13, 2017]

Some wolves were driven from the forest where they lived and hunted. Their forest was destroyed and made into a mall with a J. Crew and an Apple Store, so the wolves found another forest.

But before too long, that forest was torn down too and made into a golf course. The wolves were completely out of forest. And the wolves didn't golf.

For a time, they tried to survive in the suburbs, but there was nothing the wolves liked about the suburbs. They slept in moldy tool sheds or the backs of pickup trucks. They became gnarled and thin in the suburbs. There were no jobs there either. Even Animal Control refused to hire them to hunt raccoons and possums because the wolves were not qualified. Everyone else applying had a college education.

The wolves were forced to move towards the city. Housing was even worse for them in the city, though. Their entire pack could not find an economical way to split $3200 a month for a two bedroom. And besides, no one wanted a dog bigger than a French bulldog in any of the buildings.

Each wolf was the size of fifteen French bulldogs sewn together. They applied for public housing but were denied.

Cops tried to shoot the wolves, but they were faster than the cops. The wolves darted into the subways, sprinting through the darkened tunnels. Sometimes startled by the illuminated eye of a godspeed train, they leapt over electrified rails onto tiled platforms, and bounded up new staircases, to a different block, only to repeat it all again. More cops. More shots.

It wasn't easy on the city streets, but the wolves survived by attacking unsuspecting hot dog carts or halal trucks. Finding no natural water, the wolves developed a taste for kombucha and locally roasted organic shade-grown coffee. By Christmas Day, they were living without predators in the sewers. The quiet was worth the filth.

So they became sewer wolves, moving silently through the lowest shafts beneath the city. Each night around closing time, they would raid a dumpster outside Ray's Famous Pizza. Or burst apart the trashcans of a McDonald's. Still these wolves dreamt of blueberry skies and the ground stupid with leaves and moss. The taste of the air in the forests they had grown up in. They didn't understand opera but they hoped to.

One day, having no happiness, the wolves howled amongst themselves about how they used to enjoy stealing toddlers that were left unattended on the edge of the forest or crawling through a field of flowers, back when fields with flowers had been a thing. They howled about how they used to raise these children as their own in the forest. It used to be fun.

Sometimes the toddlers would grow into fierce warriors and be two-legged comrades to the wolves, helping them hunt and sometimes coming back to the wolf pack after a scouting mission, to sing new rock 'n' roll songs of the day.

Other times the toddlers grew up to be annoying, and the wolves could eat them for a few meals. It was a win-win.

The wolves didn't have much trouble capturing a baby. There was a park above the sewer lid and it was as easy as pushing the lid up and just nabbing a kid out of the stroller. Then, look at them all down there in the sewers, nine wolves just smiling down at a screaming baby girl covered in sewage. They were all friends right away.

The child's parents realized she was gone almost immediately but had no clue how. The police pretended they were without leads because it wasn't in their job description to have to go down into the sewers. The department of sanitation told the police it wasn't in their job description because they didn't want to battle sewer wolves. So mum was the word.

The parents hung signs all over the city. The parents put up Facebook posts. Tweets. Local TV spots. Craigslist Missed Connection: You Were Our Beloved Baby Girl And You Vanished While We Took A Selfie In Front of the Fountain, Each Day Now Our Tears Could Fill That Fountain ...

The wolves kept being wolves and life was pretty much the same for them except now they were listening to National Public Radio and were becoming increasingly liberal in their political beliefs.

Sewer Baby began to walk. Sewer Baby began to talk Wolf. In a way so alien to the human race, she flourished. Sewer Baby played with matches she found, and the wolves sang with happiness when her firelight flickered in their dense, shared darkness.

The girl's parents, having lost all hope of her return, left the city.

A forest had been cleared and a new highway opened. Seeming to sprout overnight, a house popped up for them out of the dewy sod. The family wallpapered themselves in this new house. They plastered themselves in it too. They took out a loan for a Jacuzzi and, after much trouble, had another baby. The family loved the new baby. A girl. And they named the girl the same name as the baby that had been stolen by the wolves.

Each day was a puzzle briefly shining in whatever was the sunlight.

And each night was a maze lit by mostly nothing.

And so they all forgot.

They all forgot who they were and where they'd come from.

It was too painful to remember how beautiful things had been.

Bud Smith is the author of *Teenager*, *WORK*, and *Dust Bunny City*, among others. The story "Wolves" is from the collection *Double Bird* (Maudlin House, 2018). His stories have also been at *Hobart*, *Barrelhouse*, *WhiskeyPaper*, and *The Bushwick Review*. He works heavy construction and lives in New Jersey.

Diane Williams :
Oh, Darling I'm in the Garden

[From Vol. 39 Issue 16 of the *London Review of Books*,
17 August 2017]

"Tell them all to leave. I won't look!" her husband had said.

He'd just returned from a visit to town when he said, "Tell your boyfriends to leave!"

"Oh, darling," his wife said, "I'm in the garden," and she went back outside to stand a moment near the flowering vine—the trained pillar form by the doorway.

Not today—none of the boyfriends were with her today and she felt poorly on account of it.

Nonetheless, in the salad garden, she could contemplate the bib and oak leaf and the Tom Thumb and she watered a potted plant. Then she knelt to snap off its finished blossoms and she littered the lawn with them.

On the sidewalk opposite, she saw her neighbor Mr. Timmings embracing his Affenpinscher. She left her yard, well prepared to charm either one of them.

Inside of the Timmings abode, the two forgot about the dog and worked hard to put a positive emphasis on one another. Within minutes—she found herself in the correct position, as if for sleeping—making the minor adjustments of her arms and legs as necessary.

This posture has been her salvation—and Mr. Timmings, on his knees, conjoined soon with her overhead.

Mercifully, she is free of any diseases—is intelligent, outgoing, confident—and also she tolerates hot weather reasonably well.

People who live with her admire her sympathetic nature. Although, she is not recommended for households with toddlers or small children and once she's alert, it takes her a while to settle down.

Diane Williams is the author of eight books of fiction. She is also the editor of the literary annual *NOON*. *The Collected Stories of Diane Williams* is due out fall 2018 from Soho Press.

Kevin Moffett :
Sixth Wonder

[From the anthology *We Can't Help It If We're From Florida*
(Burrow Press, 2017)]

I've been watching the nest cam again. The eaglets hatched and the mother eagle sits atop them and waits, like I wait, for the father eagle to return with a fish. On screen next to the nest cam is a live chat between a biology class and a wildlife expert. Questions appear quicker than the expert can reply to them. A student writes, Doesn't look like they made their nest right at all. And it's true, the nest does seem sort of lopsided. I used to wait for the father because when the mother moved to feed the eaglets it allowed a better look at them, wobbly and covered in gray down. Lately, I'm more interested in the father's catch. The fish is alive when he drops it into the nest and I imagine the feeling of being plucked from a river by expert talons, pulled from one element into a new one. Air, the first failure of my equipment. I bet it would feel like birth, cruel but important, and while eagles tore at my flesh, I'd be nostalgic not for the water but for the moment I was removed from it, when I flew. How had I not known I could fly? I'd be thinking.

My mother never told me storks delivered babies but she did say yes when I asked if she'd ever given a blow job. I was eight and didn't know what a blow job was—I must have overheard the phrase in school and asking if she'd given one (actually, I think I said *done* not *given*, had she ever done a blow job) was a way of asking exactly what one was. She never did tell me. For years my proxy definition of blow job was: something my mother has given, something my mother has done. To be perfectly honest the phrase blow job still conjures stubborn memory wisps of my mother. I'm thinking of her now. In the morning she'd ask my sister and me what details we remembered from our dreams, and if we said being trapped in a castle or something, she'd flip through her dream dictionary and interpret what our unconscious minds were hiding, never anything very good. Plus I could tell she left stuff out. As a teenager my sister stopped telling our mother her dreams but I never did. I started telling lies instead.

Whose little boy are you? she used to say when she was tired of me. Her eyes scanning my face without recognition, a menu of foods she didn't want in a language she didn't speak. Shouldn't you go look for your mommy?

I hated that. Whenever I remind her about it she acts like she doesn't remember. I bring it up more often than I should. My mother calls and we watch the nest cam together, her in Florida, me in California. She demands so little of me now—a phone call every two weeks, a card on her birthday, a silencing of past grievances—but I still have a hard time giving it to her. Talking to her makes me impatient, inversely annoyed with whatever she's excited about, even the nest cam. She and my sister fought over a dollhouse a few years ago and now my sister calls her that woman and rarely visits her. I never thought you'd turn out to be the normal one, my mother often tells me.

When I was in elementary school she chaperoned a trip to Blue Springs to visit our class manatee, Randy. For months we wrote him letters, but all he sent were fun facts (Fun Fact! All my teeth are molars!) and autographed photos. It's not even his signature, one of my classmates said disgustedly. We were excited anyway. When we arrived the guide pointed to a listless herd of manatees, ancient as dinosaur eggs in the clear water, and asked which was ours. Our teacher told him and the guide said, Oh, I'm so sorry. Randy died a few nights ago.

He said it with such enthusiasm I thought he was joking. He went on about industrial contaminants and the delicate ecosystem of the spring. Kids who weren't afraid to cry cried. Others stared at the manatees. For some reason I reached for my mother's hand and held it. When it became clear that we were just going to hop back on the bus and leave, my mother let go of my hand, stamped over to the guide and said, You could've pointed to any of those fat-ass manatees and said there's Randy and nobody would've known the difference.

I can't recall if he was defensive or chagrined, but neither he nor the teacher could placate her. Finally she said, We want a new one. Today. We're not going anywhere until that happens. The guide left and we sat at picnic tables and ate bag lunches, thinking about Randy and his fun facts. The guide returned a half-hour later with a picture of our new manatee, Tammy. Point her out, my mother said.

The guide indicated where Tammy was floating and told us how special she was because she'd already given birth twice. Back in class, though, Randy's picture stayed on the wall and Tammy wasn't mentioned again. What did we learn on our trip to Blue Springs? our teacher asked. No one was sure.

My mother calls in the morning to tell me that the dead fish is still in the nest with the eagles. He spent all night there, head intact, body picked clean. First, water, then air, then a crooked bed of twigs. I'm going to die without any idea what I'm capable of. This is what I'd be thinking, as eagles fed me to other eagles.

Kevin Moffett

Kevin Moffett is the author of two story collections and a collaborative novel, as well as *Sandra*, a fiction podcast cowritten with Matthew Derby and produced by Gimlet Media. His stories and essays have appeared in *McSweeney's*, *Tin House*, *American Short Fiction*, *The Believer*, *The Best American Short Stories*, and elsewhere. He has received the National Magazine Award, the Nelson Algren Award, the Pushcart Prize, and a literature fellowship from the National Endowment of the Arts. He teaches at Claremont McKenna College and in the low-residency MFA program at the University of Tampa.

Audra Kerr Brown :
The Way of the Woods

[From *F(r)Online*, August 2017]

The girls in Troop 17 found the dead baby while hunting mushrooms for their Outdoor Edibles badge. It lay at the base of a cottonwood tree, *naked and perfectly white*, they told us over a lunch of hotdogs and pudding cups. *One eye half-open.* We couldn't help but picture the groggy-looking blinds in the bunkhouse restroom.

Local police closed off the Camp Chapawee trails with yellow tape to search for clues, but they did not practice what our Scout Handbook called "The Way of the Woods." We were taught to tread softly upon the forest floor, heel-to-toe, like our Native American sisters, to crouch beneath branches instead of breaking them, to communicate with hand signals and whistles. That afternoon when we tried to earn our Bird Call badges, there was nothing to hear but the whine of ATVs and the static chirp of walkie talkies.

Scuba divers came to scour the lake bed. We worked on our Insect Classification badges as they dredged up bikini bottoms and fishing poles and piled unmatched swim flippers upon the shore like a stock of catfish.

The Camp Mothers told us not to dwell on the infant, but we were obsessed. We used our Sign Language skills, folding our arms into a cradle to say *baby*. We hadn't yet learned the sign for *dead*, so we dragged our fingers across our necks and lolled our tongues out the side of our mouths. We finger spelled the name we'd given her—K-A-T-E—after a fashion model we all longed to be, the one with the jutting cow-bone hips and sloe eyes.

The paper mache maracas we made for Music Appreciation became baby rattles. Our woven potholders for Pioneer Art were her blankets. We longed to offer them up, to honor *dead baby K-A-T-E* with Camp Chapawee respect. We wanted to build her a ceremonial fire, to chant the songs from the back pages of our Scout Handbook.

For our Constellation Identification badges we slept beneath the stars. We dreamt of willow bark papooses, dead fish, and fashion models. And when a terrible scream woke us with a start—our hearts beating furiously beneath breasts, flat and taut as deer hide drums—the Camp Mothers soothed us back to sleep, telling us not to worry. We'd soon learn for our Nocturnal Creatures badge that the wail of mating bobcats sounds just like the cry of a newborn baby.

Audra Kerr Brown lives betwixt the corn and soybean fields of southeast Iowa. Her work has appeared in *Fjords Review*, *CHEAP POP*, *People Holding*, *Fiction Southeast*, *Flash Fiction Online*, and elsewhere. She is a winner of the South Carolina Fiction Project, a two-time finalist of the Piccolo Spoleto Fiction Open, and her award-winning short story "Your Father, Frederick" was adapted into a film for the Expecting Goodness film festival. Brown earned a degree in English and Theater Arts from the University of Iowa and has studied fiction at the Iowa Writers' Workshop Summer Program.

Genevieve Plunkett :
The Buried Man

[From *Crazyhorse*, No. 91, Spring 2017]

When Barbara was a little girl, a stranger led her to a house with an odd front door. It was not a menacing stranger—more likely a family friend who had been improperly introduced. This person had walked ahead up a long, shady, sidewalk, which was cracked and mossy from the roots of old trees growing along the side. The sidewalk could have gone on and on, but they soon stopped by a section of stone wall where there was a mailbox. The stranger opened the mailbox and closed it, then motioned toward a cottage with a peculiar front door. The door was painted yellow and entombed in a very pretty front porch made entirely of glass, much like an elevator. To add to this strangeness, there was, in the middle of the cottage's driveway, a large mound of gravel. Barbara knelt in front of the mound, as if in a trance, and spread the gravel away with her hands. What she uncovered, she uncovered much faster than she would have liked. It was a pane of glass, something like the lid of a large box containing objects that became clearer as she let more light inside.

Barbara's mother denies it. She would have never left her daughter alone with a strange man, she says, which just goes to show that she has never really listened to the story. If she had, she would have known that the stranger was androgynous. All the more reason to classify it as a dream, says Barbara's father. But Barbara will not yield. It really happened, she says. How would my subconscious have created that yellow doorway? Such interesting architecture?

She had uncovered the windshield of a car. The glass was dusty, streaked by gravel and cloudy with her own handprints. If the man behind the wheel had not moved she may not have seen him at all; his brown hair and his dirty suit and tie. He did not struggle like someone buried alive, but merely looked around the interior of the car, as if he had misplaced his keys.

It was the man's movements that alarmed her; so calm and slow. Years later, when she was in her teens, Barbara went to the theater with a group of friends to see a war movie. It was a very popular movie that tried to be realistic by allowing the camera lens to be spattered with blood. In one of the battle scenes, a soldier looked down at his lap to find his organs exposed. He fondled them in disbelief, in slow, disbelieving movements. They reminded Barbara of her strange memory, of that man in the buried car, how he had just looked around. She became so uneasy that she left the theater. And as she walked up the aisle, the flickering faces all looked at her and thought, that girl is too young to see this. She should have stayed at home.

Genevieve Plunkett's stories have appeared in *The O. Henry Prize Stories*, *New England Review*, *Crazyhorse*, *West Branch*, *Massachusetts Review*, and *Willow Springs*. She lives in Vermont with her husband and two children.

Ashley Hutson :
I Will Use This Story to Tell Another Story

[From *Fanzine*, 07.19.17]

There once was a man and a dog drowning in a lake. A small crowd gathered at the water's edge.

The first person said: I should save the human, because a human life is more valuable than an animal's.

The second person said: I disagree. Humans had their chance and they blew it. They blow it every day, they're blowing it right now. Dogs, on the other hand, have that cute doggy face. Save the animal.

The third person said: I would save both, but I can't swim.

The fourth person took a photograph.

The fifth person said: In theory, I believe both the dog and the human deserve to continue living, because all life is valuable and no human should presume to hold sway on something as basic as the right to existence; however, it is obvious that both the canine and human cannot be saved simultaneously, for that is simply too much to ask of a single savior. Therefore, we must ask ourselves: what is more precious, a human life or a canine life? Shall we say human life is more important simply because we are human, and we must be loyal to our own kind? Would saving the canine be traitorous to our own species? On the other hand, humans are gifted with a conscience and are clearly running the joint (the "joint" being Earth, a little humor for you there) and so is it the human's responsibility to philosophically rise above the frail physical form into which he or she was born and commute the death sentences of other sentient species, too? Also, this argument of who may and may not bestow or take away life delightfully teases the brain regarding other arguments, too, such as: Is abortion morally wrong? What about euthanasia? What about preemptively killing the neighbor who repeatedly and believably threatens to murder a rival's family with a shotgun? Does the method of killing and level of enjoyment one derives from it matter, and if so, why? Is suicide a prosecutable offense? These arguments and thought games, drilled down to the finest nubs and ideally discussed in a spacious and beautifully furnished oak-paneled study while surrounded by rare leather-bound books, holding a brandy of an excellent year and a cigar of similarly excellent provenance—or, short of a legitimate academic setting, discussed at length on the internet, or in an impromptu Socratic forum like this one—are an important and necessary use of our time and obviously large brains. (A little more humor for you—I assure you that, as an educated person, I am well aware that the human brain's capacity for intelligence is not predicated on its physical size.) If we allow these issues to go undiscussed, how will we know that we think what we think we think? And if we don't think we think what we think we think, then how will we think clearly when action is required of us? Let's debate.

The sixth person said: Oh, look, the man and dog drowned.

The newspaper said: Tragedy, accident, nothing could be done.
The drowned man said nothing.
The drowned dog said nothing.
The lake said nothing, and it kept the bodies.

Ashley Hutson's work has appeared in *Wigleaf*, *matchbook*, *SmokeLong Quarterly*, *Catapult*, *Electric Literature*, *McSweeney's Internet Tendency*, *X-R-A-Y*, and *Split Lip Magazine*. She lives in Sharpsburg, Maryland.

Angela Mitchell :
You Are Not Like Other Children

[From *Necessary Fiction*, June 2017]

You are not like other children. You prefer to wear suits, no sweat pants, baggy shorts, shirts with team logos. You are not a slovenly child, she tells the reporter. Your model mother lifts her chin, smiles. You are the shrunken image of *him*, a father who is too old to be your father, a fact you have known since you were five and were mistaken for the child of your oldest half sister. Your wool suits, single-breasted, are made in Milan in the shades of business: black, navy, a spectrum of gray. The suits hang in a closet that is actually a room—there is a velvet sofa, a small bathroom with a sink and a golden faucet, a toilet, a refrigerator with your favorite drinks, though you are forbidden to drink them on the velvet sofa—and you have spent entire days sitting in this closet that is actually a room and no one here has questioned it. You do not like the velvet sofa—it feels, you think, too much like skin—so you sit in a far corner, beneath a dozen satin bathrobes, with your laptop. You play games with strangers online, watch videos on YouTube, download movies you are not supposed to watch. Your mother is elsewhere in the penthouse, with the man who does her hair, with the woman who circles her, up and down, with an airbrush that looks like a slender dart gun—something a spy or a hunter on safari might use—your mother naked before her. She mists her skin with a chemical that changes its color, followed by a fine coating of powder, a shimmer of crushed pearls. *This* your father insists on. You have seen photos of her when she was young, her hair dark chocolate, her face and arms and legs milky, pale. Your father's skin is old, the thickened rind of a tangerine, pink circles beneath his eyes, blue-veined and sagging. His hair is a yellow crest, fallen and flaccid, over to one side. He is gone, mostly, and you do not mind. When he is in the penthouse, he is unhappy. He paces as if in a cage, complains about this lampshade, that slab of marble, the silken fabric of the drapes. You are not like other children, but he is not like other fathers and you are not even sure how it is that you understand this. Your only explanation: he is all you have ever known.

Still, most of the time, you are left on your own, except by the servants. The one in charge of you, Irena, speaks better English than your mother, and she talks to you as she steams your suits, polishes your shoes, puts toothpaste on your brush. Irena discovers that you like M&Ms—a forbidden candy, too messy in an apartment full of white and gold—and keeps a jar of them in your closet that is actually a room, hidden behind the row of suits. You eat them in the morning, before anyone is awake, spilling them on the mahogany table beside your bed. You lean down and touch them with your tongue, one color at a time. Red, then blue, then yellow, orange, brown, red. When you do this, you are a lizard child, insects lined up before you, a feast slaughtered by your lizard mother. You do not have pets, but your school does, and your favorite is the skink, a miniature crocodile with golden scales, a sapphire leaf for a tongue. It does not lay eggs, but holds its offspring in its body until they emerge, fully formed, from beneath her tail. The teacher makes the mistake of leaving the young with her—three of them in total—and two are gone by the next morning, no remains. The mother lizard is fat again, her scales pushing out from her sides and you and your classmates look at her, at your teacher, at each other. This is strange and not so strange because haven't you suspected such a thing was possible?

But now you know everything about lizards. You sit in your closet that is actually a room and you research the blue-tongued skink, the veiled chameleon, the peacock monitor. You watch videos made by people in small houses, mismatched spaces crowded with reptile habitats. They love these lizards like their own children. What you learn is that some lizards reproduce without a partner and, by this, they do not mean that they are like fish and lay their eggs and leave them there, waiting for a male to fertilize them, but that their bodies have found a way to be both mother and father in one. You like this idea, that there need not be a father, but only the one being who makes you in her own image, releases you out into the world. The evening meal is at 9—too late for a child, but not for the 70-year-old father who demands it—and you watch your golden mother, how delicately she eats and, for a moment, you see the tip of her tongue meet the mushroom on her fork, dart back into her mouth. Her eyelids blink and you see her now, your lizard mother, the long spine of her back, her tail lost to a predator. It will grow back, but what else has she lost, what else has grown back? Beauty is different in the kingdom of lizards. What matters here is that you smell the enemy on your tongue before he arrives, that the toe you lost to a snake grows back mostly as it was, that you eat your fill when you can, fade into the rocks, the trees, the dense jungle forest, an anonymity made by your own hand. Other lizards sleep close by, secret eyes keeping watch. Alone, together, one indistinguishable from another. And you are happy. You are just like them.

Angela Mitchell's stories have been published in *Colorado Review*, *New South*, *Carve Magazine*, *storySouth*, and other journals. Her story, "Animal Lovers," was awarded the Nelligan Prize from *Colorado Review* and given special mention in *The Pushcart Prize XXXV* (35th edition, 2011). An eighth generation native of southern Missouri, she now lives in St. Louis with her husband and sons. Her short story collection, *Unnatural Habitats & Other Stories*, will be released by WTAW Press in October 2018.

Steven Dunn :
Happy Little Trees

[From *Blink-Ink #28* 2017]

Bob Ross is on. He has paint. I don't. First I grind flowers with a rock but it don't work. I chew and chew dandelions. Spit mixes into yellow paste. I chew grass. I chew mulberries. I chew wild onions. They don't make color so I swallow. Tingles back of the neck and waters my eyes. Chew coal. Chew red clay. Chew what a grasshopper chews. I chew grasshoppers. Crunchy, then juice squirts to the back of throat. The paste is chunky brown green white. Lick off hand and chew till smooth. Open jar, chew lightning bugs. Wait till night when they light, then rip off the ass, smear it on my face.

Steven Dunn is the author of two novels from Tarpaulin Sky Press: *Potted Meat* (2016) and *water & power* (2018). *Potted Meat* was short-listed for Granta's Best of Young American Novelists and a finalist for the Colorado Book Award for Literary Fiction. He is currently an MFA student at Goddard College, and some of his work can be found in *Rigorous*, *Blink-Ink*, *Columbia Journal*, and *Granta*.

W. Todd Kaneko :
B Movie

[From *Monkeybicycle*, 17 March 2017]

When I return home from the war that summer, they're looking for the Diamond. I know this because of that El Camino out front, that switchblade stuck in the coffee table, and you standing by the refrigerator in cut-off shorts and a tube top. My two uncles wonder why I'm not dead in Afghanistan. My mother cries because her boy is safe. You say, *sorry about your dad*. Later, out by the garage, we share a smoke and you say I'm handsome. I say, *you're my second cousin*. You tell me that weird story about the gypsy who told my mother I'd be dead when that log in the fireplace turned to ash, how my mother extinguished the fire and hid that log so I would return safe from the desert. The world is dangerous and I know this because of the sirens in the distance, those kids smoking dope down the alley, all that blood and pink foam when I close my eyes at night. You say, *I'm in trouble*, so we jump in that El Camino and drive south towards your father's house in Atlanta. We drive all night and into the next day with my uncles behind us because a man is the most vulnerable when he's on the road with a woman, a woman whenever she's with a man. We know this because of those two hitchhikers in their underwear, that

W. Todd Kaneko

doe bloodied and hobbling along the shoulder, your body twisting fitfully for a few hours at a Motel 6 while I dream about helicopters, snipers, and that Diamond the size of my thumb pad, eager to carve us all into pieces. When we arrive at your father's house in the morning, we are greeted by smiles and pancakes and my uncles brandishing pistols. We know we're in trouble because of their wet mustaches and your father's corpse in the kitchen. The fight is quick: two broken teeth, that shattered TV screen, three gunshots, and my uncles sprawling on the floor. I drop the gun and call my mother to explain what happened, and she cries because her boy is safe. She tells me the story about the gypsy and will continue crying for years after she hangs up because the future should be predictable. You're about to pull a gun on me. You've had the Diamond all along, and my mother is about to throw that log back on the fire. We're about to fight, you with a broken neck, me with one bullet in my gut and another in my lung. I know these things because of that gorgeous snarl you wield, because the night outside is swampy and frantic, because once in Afghanistan, I was a soldier, the only one to survive a surprise attack on his unit. The medic said, *it's okay. You're safe.* The soldier said, *no one is ever safe.*

W. Todd Kaneko is the author of *The Dead Wrestler Elegies* (Curbside Splendor, 2014) and co-author with Amorak Huey of *Poetry: A Writer's Guide and Anthology* (Bloomsbury Academic, 2018). His recent poems and prose can be seen in *The Normal School*, *Barrelhouse*, *Monkeybicycle*, *The Rumpus*, and many other places. A Kundiman fellow, he is co-editor of *Waxwing* magazine and lives in Grand Rapids, Michigan where he teaches at Grand Valley State University.

Karen Craigo :
Last Inspection of Mount Vernon by George Washington, Gentleman Farmer

[From *The Forge Literary Magazine*, Sept. 11, 2017]

At every turn on the deer path, I drop a serrated pearl.

They're the breadcrumbs of the breadless and birds eschew them. Barring more snow, this ivory should be easy to spot.

And yes, I said ivory. They were never wood. They're horse teeth and the purchased teeth of slaves. Elephant ivory. Rhino. All of it affixed to a metal frame that rests in the amphitheater of my jaw.

They cost more than a good man's house and all his holdings.

I'm feeling my years today. I'm tired. I lost my way in these woods—thought I saw something here, a presence, curious, and I stepped down from my horse and followed it in.

It ran ahead, zigzagged, behind this tree and that, and I drew nearly close enough to touch it, but no—there it was ahead, gray, a shade on the move, but in the dark, and not attached to anybody's heel.

I did not think it malevolent.

It's gone now. I thought I heard a rustling, but that was only the sound of rain hitting the canopy. Were it here, I think I'd feel it.

Listen, I know better than most how to find my way. I was a surveyor. Sometimes I feel the elemental pull of the river, and even under clouds I sense the sun. Age has dulled me, though. Deep in, all I see is green so green it's almost black, shadows that move like shadows are meant to. I unwind my way like you'd key back a clock wound too tightly, but it's no good—I'm lost here. I've passed this sycamore before. This bewildering stone. The brambles grab. Come summer they may be blackberries, or maybe the black raspberries I favor.

First I tore my cravat into strips, tied them to stems of sassafras like surrender flags. Then came the buttons, brass and shell. My greatcoat hangs open, my vest wide, my chest white as table linen.

And now I hold my mouthpiece in my hand, my old friend pain retreating.

Martha will be alarmed. She knows the care I take, my powders and my brush, the pincers the British mocked when they overtook my mail: "I now wish you would send me one of your scrapers, as my teeth stand in need of cleaning, and I have little prospect of being in Philadelphia."

And again I feel no prospect. I am dug in. This place is all I ever wanted, yet they drew me out like blood into a leech. I fought their wars, presided. I whistled through my fixture when I spoke, and so I spoke little and they thought me wise.

I won't be drawn again. I will torque myself to this land like a woodscrew to a board.

I drop a molar to mark my place and keep on moving.

Karen Craigo is the author of three poetry collections: *No More Milk* (Sundress, 2016), *Passing Through Humansville* (Sundress, 2018), and *Escaped Housewife Tries Hard to Blend In* (Tolsun Books, 2018). She is the editor-in-chief and general manager of *The Marshfield Mail* newspaper in Marshfield, Missouri, and she maintains *Better View of the Moon*, a blog on writing and creativity.

Melissa Goode :
It Falls

[From *Jellyfish Review*, Issue 25, Oct.-Nov. 2017]

We go to Berlin for a long weekend. It is February, snowing.

We visit the Memorial to the Murdered Jews of Europe. Afterwards, I return to the hotel to rest. My brain is full of numbers, starting with 2,711 grey concrete slabs.

He pulls the curtains closed. "We shouldn't have started with the memorial," he says. "We should have eased ourselves in."

"How do you ease yourself into an apocalypse?"

"We should have gone to a pub first," he says, leaving.

*

I stir at the sound of the hotel door opening. He has bought bread, cheese, and wine.

"I figured you didn't want to go out," he says.

He leans down and kisses my cheek. The evening cold comes off him. He smells of beer.

My toes are numb from walking through the snow, but that can't be possible when I have been in bed for hours. He sits on the bed and shows me photos on his phone from his walk. Snowflakes fall white and blurry past the screen, the camera capturing their fast descent, like comets with long tails.

*

We go to the Neue Wache to see the pietà sculpture *Mother with her Dead Son*.

"Is there anything sadder?" I say.

He looks at me. "Would you rather go shopping?"

I hear the irony but I say, "Yes."

We walk to Wittenberg Square and go to Kaufhaus des Westens, the "Department Store of the West." It is warm, white, clean. Bowie sings "Heroes" and even Bowie has died.

*

He buys me a woollen blue scarf that is cashmere, beyond soft, and far too expensive. While we wait in line for the cashier, he winds the scarf around and around my neck.

"You don't have to buy this for me," I say.

"I know. I want to. Okay?"

He pulls the ends tight, tighter still. I feel the pressure on my throat and I want him to pull tighter again.

*

The blue scarf is flecked with green and lilac. It makes me think of gardens, lakes, "Waterlilies," of the world in 1920 when Monet painted, rather than here in 1939-1945, or 1961-1989.

*

We eat currywurst and he tells me this is Berlin's street food. I know he'd rather we were sitting in a gutter in some tiny village in Vietnam eating wow-I-didn't-know-you-could-eat-this-species food, but we are here with chopped Bratwurst, curry powder, ketchup, and a side of fries.

*

The lights at the top of the Fernsehturm flicker red, white, red, white.

"I love television towers," I say.

He laughs. He takes my hands, blows on them, and rubs them between his gloved hands.

"Where are your gloves?" he says.

Sometimes I don't wear them when we walk because of this.

*

We go to a bar that is underground, like most cool places in Berlin. But then I think of bunkers and small, glass vials of cyanide.

"Do you think we could just have a drink?" he says.

My purple silk dress rustles when I move. His hand on my shoulder and his hip against mine, he heats the silk until it is hot, electric.

*

I touch my fingers to the window in our hotel room and it is frozen, the snow falling on the other side of the glass. He slides the zipper of my dress down slowly, all the way down my spine, and I hear it, tooth by tooth.

*

One wall of our hotel room is painted deepest, darkest red.

"I know what you're doing," he says. "You have to stop thinking about death."

I laugh. "What an extraordinary thing to say. How can I not think about it?"

"You're depressed," he says.

"Of course I fucking am. Are you living on this planet too?"

*

I stick out my tongue to taste the snow as it falls.

"How many metres do you think it fell to reach me?" I say.

"Why do you wonder about things like that?" he says.

*

In bed, I shake and shake.

He holds me. "What's wrong? I'll call an ambulance?"

My spine, my limbs, all of me moves. I cannot stop.

He puts me in the shower and I sit on the floor, my legs unsteady, hollow. My stomach is empty. He searches on his phone while holding the showerhead over me and makes the water cool, then hot, then lukewarm, then tepid.

"Everyone says something different," he says, still looking at his phone.

"What are you searching for?" I say.

"Convulsions. Fitting. Seizures. Epilepsy."

I push my face into the stream of water. It hurts — icy needles. My teeth bite and grind against each other.

"Make it hot," I say.

*

He dresses me in a T-shirt, pajama pants. He bends down in front of me, on his knees, and pulls on my socks for me. I put on his hoodie and smell him, the plane, home. I wind the scarf around my neck and my hands. He asks me in ten different ways to go to the hospital and I say no, each time.

*

We approach a church, St. Anthony's. I don't tell him that St. Anthony is the patron saint of lost things.

"I want to go inside," I say.

He looks at me. "What? Why? Is this one supposed to be good?"

He tips his head back to survey the church and I know he is evaluating architectural merit, cultural significance, relevance.

I step inside and it is quiet. There are only a few people in the pews, each with hands joined and head bowed. They are islands.

I pay one euro into the old, wooden box, and light a candle. I don't know who or what to pray for. Other candles gutter there, bright, beneath the statue of St. Mary. She is too white, Caucasian, not historically accurate. I know that.

Melissa Goode

But she watches me above the sea of candles and she is the expression of everything I want and cannot say.

Melissa Goode's work has appeared in *Wigleaf*, *SmokeLong Quarterly*, *WhiskeyPaper*, *Split Lip Magazine*, *Forge Literary Magazine*, *matchbook*, and *Jellyfish Review*, among others. One of her short stories has been made into a film by the production company Jungle. Her novel manuscript "What we have become" was selected by Random House for a fellowship with Varuna, the National Writers' House in Australia. She lives in Australia. melissagoode.com and twitter.com/melgoodewriter

Sithuraj Ponraj :
Aleppo Was Passing By

[From *Cha: An Asian Literary Journal*, Issue 35, March 2017]

a strange procession of Magi, soothsayers and children juggling neighbourhoods, edited to fit television screens.

The smiling elephants wearing polished harnesses came next with upraised grey trunks - and buildings shivered in the cold as they walked past arms clutched across the chest, foreheads flush with fever.

You had gone to fix dinner when the band walked past playing cold sirens for music while an old man in a moustache blew up the city like a blue-grey balloon.

Then grumpy grocers in pointy hats did tricks with body bags while hairdressers clapped - and a conjurer made the pavements disappear. Their faces were all burning.

I joined them when the crocodiles came out. A little girl shouted to her mother who was holding up their house on her back. Her language was all dots and slit throats.

They were still looking for the dancers when the parade suddenly ended. The people on the sidewalks cheered politely and crossed to the other side. They had waited patiently all this while.

We were busy writing posters and did not really see.

Sithuraj Ponraj writes fiction in English, Spanish, and Tamil. His first collection of short stories in Tamil, *Maariligal* won the 2016 Singapore Literature Prize for Tamil Fiction as well as the 2017 Karikaar Chozan Award in Sri Lanka for Tamil short fiction. His first collection of Tamil poetry *Kaatrai Kadanthaai* won the 2016 Singapore Literature Prize Merit Award for poetry. He has published two other novels in Tamil in 2016 and a fourth novel and a second poetry collection were published in January 2018. He also writes extensively in English. His English short fiction and poetry have been published in international journals. His first English poetry collection *The Flag Party* (Roman Books) and a chapbook *Love as a Calico Cat* will be published in 2018.

Aleksandar Hemon :
Smithereens

[From *The New Yorker*, August 30, 2017]

Near our mountain cabin, in Jahorina, there was once a hotel called Šator. It was open only in the winter for the skiing season. When you stood outside the hotel under a frigid, starry sky, you could smell cafeteria grease, wood fire, and cigarette smoke, and hear the thumping from the disco club in the basement. For the rest of the year, the hotel was vacant. One summer, when I was eleven, I broke into the hotel bar by cracking open its window—it took me an hour—and stole a bottle of blueberry juice. A guy who was a bartender there in the winter, but idled in the summer, caught me and blackmailed me, asking for money not to tell my parents. I told him to fuck off. He told my parents. They punished me, but that blueberry juice was the sweetest of potions. The hotel's cleaning staff was a woman of undetermined body shape and age, named Baja, who spent summer days sitting on the hotel balcony, looking at nothing, always wearing a blue overcoat and a black scarf on her head, one of its corners covering her jaw to keep it warm. She was, like a ghost, impervious to pain. She had an eternal toothache that she would not treat, the abscess swelling until it had devoured and destroyed one of her eyes. Nobody ever saw her clean anything, though a friend of mine who'd stayed at the hotel told me that Baja had once walked into his room without knocking, looked around, and said, "Why don't you clean this up? It's disgusting." Right behind the hotel, there was a crested boulder, which my sister and I would climb when there was nothing else to do. From the top, we could see the weekend-house cluster below and hear the buzzing of circular saws, the banging of hammers, the din of aspiration, for the weekenders were perpetually getting ready for some future in which active life would be successfully completed and there'd be nothing but peace, virginal nature, and retirement. The war would put an end to that ambition, but back then, when we were kids, the future was always on its way, its advance currents flowing through everything we knew or wanted to know. If we looked away from the house cluster, wooded vales and peaks, meadows and roads stretched toward Sarajevo and beyond, onward to the horizon, into which, at the end of the day, the sun would slide like a coin into a slot. We'd stand at the edge of the boulder, pine tips emerging from the verdant void beneath our feet, and we'd look, and look, and look: our visual field had no limits, just as our life had no end. The garbage from the hotel was dumped right behind it, down the slope at the foot of the boulder. My sister and I didn't find that strange. By the time we emerged from the unconscious part of our childhood, the world seemed fully established, everything as it was supposed to be, all the points and objects fixed, all the hierarchies and structures natural and unalterable. We'd descend from the peak to the garbage dump to browse through trash-stuffed bags and rotten food remnants. One day, we found a plethora of plates, saucers, cups, and bowls strewn all over the dump—the hotel had replaced its dishes and discarded the old ones. We spent the whole day breaking those dishes with rocks or against one another. We discussed nothing, devised no plans; it was clear to us what needed to be done. The dishes were nondescript, beige. We shattered them into smithereens, taking a break for lunch, then smashing some more in the afternoon. We sustained small cuts, but we didn't care. They were the blisters of toil, the stigmata of devotion. We discovered the pleasure of unbridled, unlimited destruction, the endless joy of converting something into nothing. This was new to us back then. Now it isn't. Now we know that that was one of the happiest days of our childhood, perhaps of our entire life. And when we went back to the dump, some time later, and found new garbage there, new generations of refuse, we knew that underneath it all were our smithereens, that we could go on forging them for as long as we were alive, that we would always remember the day we first broke the limited whole.

Aleksandar Hemon's books include the novels *The Making of Zombie Wars, The Lazarus Project,* and *Nowhere Man,* and the story collections *The Question of Bruno* and *Love and Obstacles.* Born in Sarajevo, Bosnia and Herzegovina, in 1964, Hemon was visiting the United States in 1992 when the Bosnian War broke out, whereupon he settled in Chicago. Hemon was awarded a Guggenheim Fellowship in 2003, and received a MacArthur "genius grant" the following year. He has also worked as a screenwriter, most recently on the Netflix show *Sense8.* "Smithereens" is from his forthcoming book *This Does Not Belong to You* (FSG).

Raul Palma :
Filthy, Polluted

[From *SmokeLong Quarterly*, Issue Fifty-Eight, December 18, 2017]

At daybreak, when your mother brings you a café con leche, then asks if you have a moment, slide a chair over and say, "For you. Always."

She doesn't need to know the ins-and-outs of the ongoing investigation, all the ways your brother incriminated the family. She doesn't need to know that everything is on the line: the house, the cheap festival artwork, the view of the golf course.

Lie because your mother deserves better, this miracle of a woman who survived Cuba's special period only because, starving, she placed her family and her faith in the expanse of the Florida Straits—a woman, widowed, who sits before you in the very gown she wore to sea, her only Cuban possession, washed so many times it's as frail as a tissue.

When she tells you that there were brothers before you, don't follow up with a question. Listen. Allow her to unfurl the photo album, pictures of two little boys, treasured—wild boys with sticks in their hands and ash streaks across their faces; boys, who in one photo, seem tucked into bed. No. On that yellowed photo paper, they're dead. Imagine them beneath the ground that way, tucked in caskets, wait your mother to awaken them with her confession.

Find her on the lanai, peeling a mango with a small knife, letting the juice drip off her elbow and onto the pavers you just had pressure cleaned. When she cuts you a piece of the fruit, offers with the knife, don't eat it—her little slice of sunshine, fruit from Publix, but which might as well be from el campo, the hundred-year-old tree in Guanajay that she'd sit under as a child, where, learning to crawl, she'd drag herself towards the fallen fruit to suckle among the flies.

Instead, tell her "What am I supposed to do with this information, Ma?"

Then, feeling your indignation, let her have it, but know that she will not hear your words; this woman, who has survived a dozen hurricanes, will only feel the breeze on her skin.

Raul Palma is an Assistant Professor of Writing at Ithaca College. He holds a PhD in English from the University of Nebraska-Lincoln, where he also specialized in ethnic studies. Most recently, his work appeared in *Alaska Quarterly Review*, *SmokeLong Quarterly*, and *Sonora Review*. His fiction was distinguished/notable in *The Best American Short Stories 2016*, and it has been supported with fellowships and scholarships from the CubaOne Foundation, the Kimmel Harding Nelson Center, the Santa Fe Writers Conference, Sewanee Writers' Conference, Sundress Academy for the Arts, and Ithaca College. He serves as fiction editor for *Prairie Schooner*.

Cristoph Keller :
Knowledge

[From *SAND Journal*, Issue 15, 2017]

I don't have to tell you that Trishna believes everything about God. It worries me that she might have heard of the early gnostic Basilides who said what defines God is that he is not. Can you find out whether she's aware of this? Please be gentle.

Christoph Keller (1963) born in Switzerland, dividing his time between New York and St. Gallen, Switzerland, and writing in German and English, is the author of numerous prize-winning novels, plays, and essays in German, including *Gulp* (1988); *I'd Like My Country Flat* (1996), and *The Stone Eye* (2016); and the best-selling memoir *The Best Dancer* (2003). The most recent titles are *We're On: A June Jordan Reader*, co-edited with Jan Heller Levi (Alice James Books, 2017), *A Meaningful Life 2.0*, short prose (Birutjatio, 2018) and *Hip Hops: Poems about Beer* (Everyman's Library Pocket Poets, 2018). christophkeller.us

Lauren S. Marcus :
The Collector

[From *Into the Void Magazine*, Issue 5, Autumn 2017]

My father rummages through our neighbours' garbage for recyclables. Once a month, he drives miles to redeem them for cash, bulging bags bouncing around his car, pounds and pounds in exchange for twenty-three dollars. His eyes see treasure everywhere—the battered cabinet on the side of the road, the overturned shopping cart in an alley, rotting books in a gutter. They are all carefully harvested and brought back to the garage, where they sit forever, waiting.

My brother and I ask why he collects trash. It's worthless stuff, we tell him.

He is angry. We might need it one day, he snaps, it might be worth something. When we need it, and we don't have it, then, we would be sorry.

Wild black hair, unmistakably curly no matter how short he keeps it, crowns his head. He always wears long sleeves, despite the Los Angeles heat, lest—*khas v'khalila*—his olive skin darken any deeper. His forearms are fuzzy with black fur. A stubborn wave of black chest hair crests at the collar of his shirt. Dark, almond-shaped eyes live deep in his wrinkled face, protected by bushy brows and long lashes. But most importantly: his nose, broad and hooked, with a bump for good measure. A nose so evocative of far away places that my father is constantly approached in foreign tongues—Armenian, Arabic, Hebrew, Farsi, each speaker convinced my father is from their homeland.

My brother and I are fair-skinned and blue-eyed and small-nosed. My father is grateful for this and tells us so. We look goyish, he says with a smile, like cherubs on a Vatican ceiling, like angels hanging from a Christmas tree.

It's important to blend in, he says.

In restaurants, he empties napkins from dispensers, folding them neatly and sliding them into his pockets. Condiments are next, packets of mustard and ketchup, little plastic tubs of pickles, then entire jars of hot sauce, which he wraps in a plastic bag he asks for at the counter. In hotels, the maid's cart sitting in the hallway stands no chance against him—he walks out of our room with a pillow case and fills it to the brim with mini-bottles of shampoo, body wash, Listerine.

He is an insomniac. One night, I find him in the living room at four a.m., sitting his personal shiva, his strange treasures scattered around him. He is arranging them: the back issues of *National Geographic*, chipped china plates, salt and pepper shakers made to look like dinosaurs. He looks up at me, irate, as though I've challenged his reign over this peculiar kingdom. I back out of the room without saying anything.

I am engaged to a kind man. I try to warn him. My dad is a little out there, I say. He fills our home with junk. My fiancé asks why. He had to flee two countries, I say. He didn't speak the language. He lost everything. Twice. My fiancé says he understands. It's impossible that he understands—even I can't.

You're a survivor, my fiancé says to my father.

My father frowns. After a long time, he says, No.

Lauren S. Marcus is a writer and journalist based in Tel Aviv. Her work has appeared in *The Jerusalem Post*, *The Forward*, and *+972Magazine*, among other publications. laurensmarcus.com

Robert Long Foreman :
Weird Pig

[From *Copper Nickel*, Spring 17, Issue 24]

Weird Pig went to the grocery store, to look for softer mud. All he found was sand for a sandbox he didn't have. He was caught on camera, eating marshmallows in Aisle 8 straight from the bag. After a brief confrontation, he left the store snorting, vowing never to return.

Weird Pig wasn't so weird. In a lot of ways he was just like you and me. He was afraid to die, but mostly seemed to pretend it wouldn't happen to him. He didn't like the scene in *Last Tango in Paris* where Marlon Brando tells that poor woman she should have sex with the pig that throws up on people.

He remembered when the wars in Iraq and Afghanistan began, but in his heart he felt certain he would not see them end. War was a burden on the conscience of Weird Pig's generation, and it would be on his piglets' generation's conscience, too.

Oh, yes. Weird Pig was a dad.

He fell in love with Nancy Pig, who gave birth to a whole litter. Farmer Dan hollered with joy, and so did Weird Pig.

But there was one little piglet who didn't fare well. Stillborn, Farmer Dan called him. Stillborn Pig. He was one of seven pigs born that day, and the only one who didn't make it, but Weird Pig felt a part of him die when he saw Stillborn Pig's wet corpse in the straw.

They buried him behind the barn. There was no ceremony.

Weird Pig got solemn. Weird Pig drank, hiding his stash of rum behind the trough. Someone always seemed to find it, then leave it sitting out so that Weird Pig would see it there and know it had been found. They never discussed it, he and whoever it was who left it there, probably Nancy Pig. Definitely Nancy Pig.

Weird Pig was a jolly drunk, mostly, as pigs tend to be. But there was often a point in the night when for no reason Weird Pig got quiet. He got morose. He stopped making eye contact with his buddies, Jake Rooster and Bill Wyman the Mule. The laughter ran dry.

Weird Pig yelled at the piglets when he came home on the worst night he'd had in a long time. Nancy Pig pulled them close, as if to shield them from his words. He said there was no such thing as Flying Pig, which of course was true, but is not something you should dump on a piglet's head in a rage. It's cruel. Weird Pig stormed out. Nancy Pig squealed after him. He slept in the field, and when he woke up, blinking at the unforgiving sun, he heard the laughter of the Crows, Diane and Marcus Crow.

The piglets were quiet when Weird Pig stumbled in, sometime later. They didn't look at him, but Nancy Pig watched in silence as he went to the trough for some water. Nancy wished they could have their old life back. The piglets only wished he would leave.

Weird Pig saw his reflection in the trough. What he saw he hardly recognized as Weird Pig.

He turned to Nancy with tears in his eyes. He couldn't speak. He oinked with sorrow.

There was hope, though. Nancy fed him slop, talked sense into him, made him agree to drink only in moderation, no more than three nights a week.

It didn't work. A month later, after another bad night, it was clear that Weird Pig couldn't handle any drinking at all. He joined a support group at Dan's church, where at his first meeting he opened up about Stillborn Pig, and told everyone his fear of being slaughtered and eaten. They applauded him for his honesty, and he got a sponsor: Field Hand Rick.

Weird Pig stayed clean ever after. He was a model father, adored by his piglets. Nancy Pig could not have been happier. One Christmas, Nancy Pig bought presents for each of the piglets, and Weird Pig was slaughtered so that Farmer Dan and his own offspring, Kid Bryce and Girl Pearl, could eat Weird Pig off of plates. Later, to pay for college, they went into lifetimes of debt, and Weird Pig was nothing more than the distant memory of a Christmas dinner eaten on a farm where after dinner Kid Bryce wrote a poem that went,

Thank you, Weird Pig, thank you so,
For the meat you have provided,
You've helped my arms and legs to grow
And our hunger has subsided.

It was amateur work by a well-fed but poorly educated child. It was thrown away by Farmer Dan, who thought poetry was the work of homosexuals. He forbade Kid Bryce from writing more of it.

The farm isn't there anymore. It was demolished to make way for an industrial livestock production facility, which has lots more pigs in it than the farm did. There are so many pigs, they don't even clean up all the shit that comes out of them. They just give the pigs antibiotics so they don't get infections from wading through their own waste all day.

Farmer Dan got a job working security at the grocery store. He doesn't know it yet, but he has bowel cancer, and won't live to see Kid Bryce become a man. Oh, Farmer Dan.

Robert Long Foreman's first book is *Among Other Things* (Pleiades Press, 2017). His work has appeared in magazines like *Crazyhorse*, *Cincinnati Review*, and *Agni*. He is finishing work on a novel about Weird Pig, and you can find more stories about Weird Pig, and things he has written that aren't about Weird Pig, at robertlongforeman.com. He lives in Kansas City.

Kathleen Jones :
The Exact Coordinates of Eleanor

[From *Paper Darts*, July 13, 2017]

Eleanor made sure she was drunk for the moon landing. Downed three shots of whiskey alone in the kitchen. In the bathroom, she swished Listerine, spat into the sink.

Helen already stood at the front door with Eleanor's mother-in-law, Martine. "Let's go!" Eleanor said brightly, locking the door behind them because Martine would complain if she didn't. They walked down the block. The whiskey bloomed.

The Hendersons were snobs, but they offered television, a big living room, cocktails and canapes. Helen perched on a sofa; Eleanor sat beside her on the carpeted floor. Her hand nudged a narrow wooden sofa leg, her fingers landing in a crevice of hair and grit. A man spoke of coordinates and space dust, and Eleanor transferred her fingertips to Helen's ankle.

"It isn't real," crowed Martine. "It's theater!" Everyone in the neighborhood looked at her, aghast.

Eleanor wasn't embarrassed. Martine didn't know anything; she'd seen her son in a casket but didn't believe he was dead. There was a moon, and there was almost a man on it, there was dirt in space and dirt on her hand, and even the living room—so far below—had an orbit and a taste and a plan.

Kathleen Jones is a writer of poetry, fiction, and technical documentation. She lives in Wilmington, North Carolina, and holds an MFA in Poetry from the University of North Carolina Wilmington. Her work is forthcoming from *IDK Magazine* and *North Carolina Literary Review*, and can be found in *Grist Online*, *Rust + Moth*, *Meridian*, and others. Find her on Twitter @kathleenejones.

Deb Olin Unferth :
37 Seconds

[From *Wait Till You See Me Dance* (Graywolf Press, 2017). The story originally appeared in *Columbia: A Journal of Literature and Art*]

1. The time it takes for her to verify the problem.
2. For him to say that it isn't his fault, and for her to cry out, Well, it isn't hers either.
3. (Mango falls in the field nearby.)
4. The time it takes for her to dig once more through her bag,
5. to gather the documents, to count them,
6. to attempt to account for the missing one,
7. to arrange them in a pile,
8. to lament their disarray.
9. For a longing look at the other side of the border: scrub trees, cactus bush, the green of a brown mountain, of a white sky.
10. To consider going back, forgetting the whole thing.
11. His next suggestion, not a perfect one, but . . .
12. Her complaint: "You never understand *anything!*"
13. Both of them, brooding.
14. For her to consent to his plan even though it won't work. She knows what will happen. She speaks the language, after all, not he.

15. The slow walk to the kiosk.
16. For her to lean over the counter, speak into the little mouth cup in the glass,
17. to shove the stack of papers into the slot,
18. to retrieve a paper fallen to the ground, to catch the other ones slipping.
19. The length of her explanation, her supplication,
20. meanwhile he in a patch of dry grass, observing.
21. For the lady to reject their application.
22. The slow walk from the kiosk.
23. For a pause to glance back, to see the vendors over the border—she can see them from here—a man selling blankets, copper mirrors, a woman selling rings.
24. Seventy thumps in the chest between them. What are they going to do now?
25. Eighty thumps in the chest between them. Their trip, ruined!
26. The emergence of a cramp behind his left eye.
27. The emergence of a thought in her mind, the suppression of it, its reemergence,
28. the contemplation of it: it's his fault!
29. He was supposed to be in charge of the documents. He had one small job—
30. Not enough time to figure out what he could reasonably say, but less time than it takes to have said it, heard a response, and shouted something else.
31. For her to recite a list, another list, of other things he has forgotten on other trips, and elsewhere, beginning with aspirin, ending with umbrella, and all the items in between—birthdays, promises, punch lines.
32. Four blinks from him, seven from her (watery eyes).
33. For it to register that he is insulted, for him to comment on the insult, that he is insulted like this often.
34. (A vulture drifts by overhead. Mountains, low red sky.)

35. The time it takes to go from being depossessed to repossessed (as in: car) of the missing document. He suddenly remembers it's in his suitcase.
36. Or decompressed, an exhalation of relief (as in: air mattress),
37. or pressed (olives), two halves of a suitcase back together,
38. or possessed by an urge to forgive,
39. or compressed (as in: compression of the brain [1% compression of a brain]), any lingering resentments, squashed, shoved down in there hard.
40. The apology (forlorn cows standing around, military police a few meters off): she didn't mean it, she loves him, he is wanted.
41. The slow walk back to the kiosk.
42. To place a happy coin in the palm of a nearby boy.
43. The sight of two tourists limping off before the boy looks away.

Deb Olin Unferth is the author of five books, including the story collection *Wait Till You See Me Dance* (Graywolf Press, 2017). Her work has appeared in *Harper's*, *The Paris Review*, *Granta*, *Vice*, *Tin House*, the *New York Times*, *NOON*, and *McSweeney's*. An associate professor at the University of Texas in Austin, she also runs the Pen-City Writers, a creative writing program at the John B. Connally Unit, a penitentiary in southern Texas.

Michael Parker :
Deep Eddy

[From *Everything, Then and Since* (Bull City Press, 2017).
The story originally appeared in *Southwest Review*]

We had to park by the bridge where the black ladies fished through dusk on upturned plastic buckets, ignoring us as they peered into the murk for the bob of red cork in the water. A quarter-mile walk along a root-ruptured path to where the water whirlpooled and the bottom dropped so wildly, myth bubbled up from it, a froth of dead babies crying on moon-shiny nights, suicide pacts of numerous young lovers, an entire stagecoach of painted ladies, midway from Charleston to Baltimore in pursuit of a regiment of whoremongers, sucked under its current. Sorcery, devilment, human sacrifice: legends spread for decades by teenagers who heard them from grandmothers trying any old lie to warn them away from a place known for deflowering. But we went that night and other nights seeking only the wild circling current. We'd just been to see a movie where a dingo ate a baby, stole it from a tent in the night while the parents slept alongside it, and we were talking all Australian. Bye-bee, she called me, my bye-bee. We went in with our underwear on, laughing at our awful accents. She'd lost her flower with the first of a string of boys and she liked me only in the way girls like those boys who make them forget, temporarily, some pain I hoped was only temporary. My job was to make her laugh. So we laughed at babies carted off by dogs on big grainy screens; we mocked the fantastic rumors of that cow-licked spot in the river and dubbed it Jacuzzi, we laughed at the word Jacuzzi, hollered it into the dark woods so we could laugh again at the echo. But the word rang in my head until it was frightening, not funny, so I told her something true that I knew she might misinterpret as the first line of a joke. Today I saw part of a snake. If she said, What part? I would swim to shore, pull on my clothes and leave. If she just said, Which? I would stop fighting the current and allow it to deliver me to her. Everything—then and since—hinged on a single word. There was no answer, just a gurgling in the dark water, laughter from the eternal circle of poor drowned whores, the baby in the dingo den, the short end of the snake.

Michael Parker is the author of six novels and three books of stories and is a three-time winner of the O. Henry Award. A new novel, *Only the Horse Knew the Way*, will be published by Algonquin in spring 2019. He is the Vacc Distinguished Professor in the MFA Writing Program at University of North Carolina at Greensboro, and lives in Saxapahaw, North Carolina and Austin, Texas.

Michael Parker :
How to Be a Man

[From *Everything, Then and Since* (Bull City Press, 2017)]

When he was in high school, the boy took a job in the after-
noons and on weekends at a drugstore. The alcoholic phar-
macist yelled at him for things like being sixteen and not
knowing how to back a trailer or put water in a car battery.
He could not squeegee the windows worth a damn, and the
one time he was allowed to run the register, it came up just
shy a dollar. Go clean the items in the window, the pharma-
cist said to him one afternoon, and the boy took a dust rag to
the wheelchairs, canes, walkers, and other medical supplies
staged on the platform by the plate glass. The arrangement
of the items bothered him; he was prone to moving the
furniture around in his bedroom every few months so that
he could walk into the room and feel like he'd never been in
it before, or that it belonged to someone else, someone with
vision and options. Once he even took the sliding doors off
his closet and pushed the head of his bed against the wall,
and he did not even mind when he woke to a nightmare of
jungle and vine, only to realize he was being grazed by the
cuffs of his Sunday trousers. Lying in bed among belts and
neckties hanging from coat hangers made him feel he was
living in a city, in an apartment so small he had no choice

but to put his bed in a closet, far from his parents and the pharmacist. He wanted to transform the window of the drugstore into something similarly fresh and disorienting, but there wasn't much to work with. It wasn't fully possible to arrange the merchandise in such a way that did not say to people on the street, Not only are you going to die, but we are going to make some money off your demise. But in order to create the opposite emotion he felt when he woke with his head in a closet, he would have to leave everything the way it was, the way it had been since he'd taken this job, probably since the drugstore first opened its doors. And now the boy felt stuck: he did not like the pharmacist and he did not want him to make any money at all, much less profit off of the elderly and infirm, but leaving things the way they were, depriving the world of the spark of renewal, seemed to him equally distasteful. And so, seized with an anxiety that produced in him not jitters but lassitude, he sat down in a wheelchair to try and think what to do. The pharmacist must have been busy or drinking with his buddies in the stock room, for an hour passed and the boy sat undisturbed in the wheelchair, struggling with the confusion of his desires as outside people passed by without a glance his way. And he hated them for it, and he loved them for it, too.

Michael Parker is the author of six novels and three books of stories and is a three-time winner of the O. Henry Award. A new novel, *Only the Horse Knew the Way*, will be published by Algonquin in spring 2019. He is the Vacc Distinguished Professor in the MFA Writing Program at University of North Carolina at Greensboro, and lives in Saxapahaw, North Carolina and Austin, Texas.

Jan Stinchcomb :
Uncouple

[From *matchbook*, March 2017]

She got into his car because all sedans are the same in the dark but she wasn't his wife and he wasn't her husband. He had a moment of terror as he saw her green eyes light up. He smelled her perfume. She appeared completely ready.

In the first days they drove for hours. Instead of hotels they chose amusement parks and movie theaters. Instead of sex they reveled in not answering to anyone, not belonging anywhere. They ate popcorn for dinner and chocolate for breakfast. They felt as though they had returned to toddler-hood, a free fall of the id with an assumed safety net. After all they were two decent people. He would not let her do anything rash. She would not let him hurt himself.

You remind me of my wife, he said. Just a little.

You are nothing like my husband.

At night they slept on the beach. Occasionally their children would join them and then their spouses, who approached with the exquisite caution of wildlife photographers.

It looks as though they're doing a good job, he whispered.

Let's get out of here, she said.

He did not know where to go. Covered in sand they drove to the nearest neighborhood and walked into the first house they saw, which was white with black trim, punctuated by Cape Cod windows. They wandered through the rooms and up the stairs, peeking into drawers and closets, the dread creeping up his ribcage. When he could no longer stand the suspense he escaped to the backyard.

She waved at him from the master bedroom balcony. The family who could lay claim to those Cape Cod windows had returned home, jingling keys and calling out to each other but she was unconcerned. He knew himself to be an intruder while she remained still and serene. He wished the damp soil, already claiming his heels, would take all of him. Soon the mother and the father who lived at the house were standing on the balcony alongside his accomplice, as he thought of her, and before long the three of them were talking and smiling.

She has made herself acceptable, he thought. Somehow she is not a threat to them.

I could never be like you, he confessed when they were back in the car, driving off to a neighborhood in the hills with seductive views of the ocean. He wasn't sure if he had enough gas.

I've been doing you a favor, she told him.

He protested that he had not even kissed her but he did not want to fight. He wanted to hang on.

She blew a kiss into the air.

Look, she said, pointing. Look how loosely everything is held together. Drop me off over there, she told him, nodding at a sedan parked under a canopy of jacarandas. They were in the heart of the hills now. In the car sat another man, looking down, as yet untroubled.

Jan Stinchcomb is the author of *The Blood Trail* (Red Bird Chapbooks, 2018) and *Find the Girl* (Main Street Rag, 2015). Her stories have recently appeared in *Black Candies: The Eighties*, *WhiskeyPaper*, *Atticus Review*, and *Monkeybicycle*, among other places. She is a reader for *Paper Darts*. Currently living in Southern California with her husband and children, she can be found on Twitter @janstinchcomb. janstinchcomb.com

Giovanna Varela :
Surf Jesus

[From *Southern Indiana Review*, Fall 2017]

The Surfer guides a pineapple through a circular saw, and the fruit splits open like slippery bark under boot and axe. She rubs the juice onto her hand—a gory parable feeding wood and plaster to electric metal teeth. Glazing the bloody yellow wedge onto her open palm, she imagines how the afternoon will go: Surf Jesus will walk up fresh from a session—his board bruised and wet like the underside of his tongue. She'll listen to him talk about his Christian death metal band, and he'll watch her work, correcting her misplaced hands. Surf Jesus will gum bare lacquer to create marbled glass pipes. Blaze and praise, he'll say. The Surfer will carve Cocoa Beach in Art Deco font on Surf Jesus' chest with a butterfly switchblade, and they'll share a plate of whiskey-cake and shrimp on the hood of her sunset pink Camaro. Under a darkening sky, swirled purple and orange like a jawbreaker, they'll split a bottle of malt liquor like teenagers at a pet cemetery and talk about optimum ways to die: close to home, in the dark, under a swell.

Surf Jesus shows up earlier than expected and the Surfer's just standing there, chewing on pineapple rind, unaware of the blood and juice running down her arm, curling like a rope around her ankle.

Giovanna Varela grew up in Central Florida, and her work is influenced by her home region. She is a candidate in two MFA programs: creative writing at The New School, and film production at Emerson College. She is the winner of *Big Muddy*'s 2017 Mighty River Short Story Contest, and her fiction has also appeared in *FOLIO*, *Literary Juice*, *Rock & Sling*, *Owen Wister Review*, *Southern Indiana Review*, and *Moon City Review*. Giovanna is currently working on her experimental documentary on Orlando-Kissimmee, and a short story collection called *Flamingo City*.

Ruth LeFaive :
Clean Girls

[From *Split Lip Magazine*, November 2017]

Caitlin enunciates the words mother and kitchen and
mopping like each syllable has scrubbing properties, like
she's flossing with vowels, cleaning her mouth out for Mr.
Gilcrest, our drama teacher. She hopes he'll notice her
A-plus-elocution and become her love slave. She's telling
us again about the time, years ago, when she first learned
about blow jobs, the day a neighbor kid was all blow job
this and blow job that. Janet Rossmore lurks two seats up.
We can smell her cigarettes and greasy hair from here, and
we know she's listening. Everybody's listening. Caitlin gets
to the part where she asked the kid what a blow job was
and he said, "Go ask your mother." Her mom was in the
kitchen mopping. Caitlin pauses for suspense and gets into
character: college graduate relegated to domestic labor in a
cluttered suburban ranch home. She raises her wrist to her
forehead (keeping her other hand on the invisible mop),
exhales and mimics, "Some people—not me, but some—
find it pleasurable to suck on a man's penis." Caitlin drops
the invisible mop and becomes herself again. She says at
first she had envisioned a lone penis, like that song every-
body's parents hate. "Detachable Penis." We laugh with her

about this. We picture groceries: popsicles and éclairs. Rolls of Life Savers, only bigger. One of us giggles, "Jar of penis, Aisle 12!" But Caitlin has stopped laughing. Her performance is finished. She zips her backpack and waits for the bell to ring. We all wait, and although the lull is short, it's long enough to imagine the some people. We see them on their knees and we think of Janet Rossmore—we don't know why. We remember how she never washed her face at camp last summer. Each morning while we brushed our teeth at the row of sinks and mirrors, chatting with foaming mouths, Janet stood alone and quiet, adding eyeshadow to her lids, covering the smudges from the day before.

Ruth LeFaive is a writer in Los Angeles. Her work has appeared in *Atticus Review*, *CHEAP POP*, *The Offing*, *Split Lip Magazine*, and elsewhere. She is currently working on a collection of linked short fiction.

Nancy Au :
She Is a Battleground

[From *Lunch Ticket*, Issue 11, Summer/Fall 2017]

Twelve-year-old butter boys face the old Chinese woman they call Baboochka. Imagine: the eighty-year-old woman on their apartment's shared front stoop, the silver moon caught in her tousled hair, her yellow sweater vest, her milky-white Velcro E-Z Steppers. She jostles grocery bags from one hip to the other as she digs in her pockets for keys. She grumbles about the checker at the vegetable market pocketing her change, about her arthritic fingers too weak to open jars but too strong for the wet lettuce bag, about the bus driver that did not hear her call out for a stop. And now, the butter boys on her stoop who whistle for sesame candy, beg to see inside her bags, throw dirty leaves in her hair when she refuses.

The old woman knows that in two years the boys will become teenage fools: lanky legs, smelling, soiled under-pants, an erection when someone taps their shoulder or sloshes in a puddle or fires a gun. It doesn't take much. The fools will come home from school and find the old woman weaving long green blades of grass into her house slippers like laces, her purse filled with acorns, resting against her stockinged feet. The fools will laugh and point their sticky fingers at Baboochka, some so close they leave fingerprints on her eyeglasses.

And the old woman will choose to fight back. In her own true myth, she is not a corny grandmother, soft like a pillow. She is not Mother Dear. She is not Lady Khorosho, just waiting to become a ghost. She does not weep and cry and mumble. No.

She is a battleground. Lui yun is her real name, she will tell the fools, Go and puk gai. She is a person. She is sex. She is useful poison. She is a survivor of wars. She is a dream. She is a sarcastic beast. She is the skeleton key who understands little criminals. She will yank the fools' earlobes with joy, grab handfuls of shirt and rip them a new hemline.

And the arrogant snots will call her mad, crazy, a shithead, a starry buttock, a whore. But the old woman will laugh and laugh, howl like a bolshy dame. The sound, quick, scratching, the sweetest noise you've ever heard. Like an ancient drug, with chipped teeth like tin bells, a tongue like a rake, a fighting drive to live, a horror heart in woolly slippers.

Nancy Au's stories appear in *Lunch Ticket*, *Tahoma Literary Review*, *The Pinch*, *Pithead Chapel*, *Beloit Fiction Journal*, *SmokeLong Quarterly*, *Mary Journal*, *Liminal Stories*, *Jellyfish Review*, *Forge Literary Magazine*, *Foglifter*, *Midnight Breakfast*, *Identity Theory*, *FRiGG*, among others. She has an MFA from San Francisco State University. She teaches creative writing (to biology majors!) at California State University Stanislaus, and is co-founder of The Escapery, a writing and art unschool (www.theescapery.org). She is a four-time nominee for *The Best Small Fictions* (2017-2018), and her flash nonfiction is nominated for Best of the Net (2018). peascarrots.com

Jessica Walker :
Ex-Utero

[From *Reservoir*, Issue III, January 2017]

I am two weeks post-op, plunging a toothpick toward a cocktail wiener, when I wish my mother never put those nasty little sausages on the coffee table. My toothpick hits an empty plate where the food used to be.

My mother is flipping through the channels, deciding which New Year's Eve show to watch. My cousin Vera is on the couch breastfeeding Baby Davey. Her step-son Kevin is staring at my tits. Davey lifts his head, looks at me accusingly.

Fuck you, Davey, I mouth silently.

Baby Davey gets it, goes back to the teat.

*

The tumor in my uterus was as large as my head, like a seven-month fetus. The hospital forms required a designated driver to pick me up. I listed my mother. The forms listed my age: thirty-five. The medical staff looked at me sad. But not as sad as they looked at me after the hemorrhaging, after the emergency hysterectomy. I got extra pudding. Unlimited morphine. So much sympathy in the room over what was gone, my body barely fit.

*

My mother has noticed the missing wieners.

"Marlena, did you eat this entire plate?"

"No."

"As a woman, I know this is hard. But you can't bury the pain in sausage. You'll ruin your figure."

"Maybe it was Kevin. He looks stoned."

I head Kevin's way until his body spray, cigarette stench, and leering are too close to bear.

"Got any weed?" I ask.

On the back porch, Kevin hands me a joint.

"So, it is true you can't have kids and shit?" he asks.

"What's it to you?" I take a hit.

"I like a girl who ain't got her parts. Can't get pregnant and you got no period."

I wish what I've wished ever since Vera met her new husband—that Kevin would drop off the face of the earth. And he's gone. A passing train rumbles the house. I've timed my life by the railroad schedule. This should be the last one of the year.

*

The surgery was the week before Christmas. I didn't want my mother there. She made me nervous. So she dropped me off and picked me up, the bare requirements under hospital policy.

When she came to get me, I was doped up. I told the truth.

"The tumor's gone!"

"Oh baby!"

"My uterus is gone!"

"Oh, baby."

In the hospital lobby, she stopped at a plastic manger scene, grabbed the Jesus figure and forced him in my robe pocket.

"It's ours," she said. "A miracle baby."

I fumbled my hand in my pocket, felt how light, how hollow it was. On the way out, I tossed it into a snow-covered flower bed. Jesus sunk.

*

Everyone is obsessed with Kevin's whereabouts. Baby Davey looks at me accusingly. I'm beginning to think he senses my new ability, that he's got infant ESP, wisdom of the womb lingering like the jaundice and fragment of umbilical cord he can't seem to shake.

"Did he say anything?" Vera asks. "Did he get a call? Did you see what direction he went?"

"Don't worry about that kid," I say. "He always comes back, like herpes."

Vera covers Baby Davey's ears.

"Marlena!" my mother says. "What's gotten into you?"

"A tumor is what got into me. Not that you care. All you care about is what's gone out of me."

"Don't lose hope," Vera says. "There's adoption! Stepkids! One doctor said I'd never be a mother. Now look at me."

Baby Davey is chomping on her nipple and his stink wafts toward me. I can see bruises darkening Vera's breast. I know that beneath our soft waistbands we have the same incision. She bore a child; she's a hero. I begat a tumor; it's something we don't talk about. I get no credit for surviving my own life, only pity I can't create another.

*

A few days ago, I went back to the hospital. On the way inside, I saw the plastic legs of Baby Jesus poking through the snow. If I could bend over, if my abdomen weren't patched together with stitches and glue, I would have returned him to the manger. He wasn't altogether bad. He just wasn't the thing for me.

The tumor was benign. The doctor asked if I had discomfort. I said yes, that I was in pain, that I was weak, that I didn't feel like I was in the same body.

You're not the same, the doctor said, but the weakness and pain will pass.

Beneath my incision I felt movement—an itch and a wiggle in the hollow space where life and death could grow. I wished for stillness. The wiggle disappeared.

*

I tell my mother and Vera: "I don't want a kid. Never have."

"Science has come a long way," my mother says. "I saw a thing about a uterus transplant on TV—"

"Oh God. I wish you'd just go away."

My mother and Vera vanish. The cocktail wieners reappear. Alone on the couch, Baby Davey looks at me accusingly, again. I tell him they won't be gone forever, that this is a blessing—a moment of our own. We have to find peace where we can. I strip off my sweatpants—they're itching my incision. I eat wieners, watch TV, wait for the ball to drop.

A rumble climbs to a roar. There is one more train. I take Baby Davey outside. The vibrations shake the house, then fade to nothing. Davey grabs and gulps for milk I don't have. I show him things no one else will—tracks that lead away, my scar, how to spell our names in the stars.

Jessica Walker is an MFA candidate at the University of Virginia and the winner of *Bayou Magazine*'s James Knudsen Prize. Her short stories can be found in publications such as *Indiana Review*, *Bayou*, *Booth*, and *Ninth Letter Online*. She is at work on her first novel.

Melissa Lozada-Olivia :
House Call

[From *Aster(ix)*, Dirty Laundry, Fall 2017]

katharine is getting her monthly brazilian wax $$ she isn't
seeing anyone $$ so this isn't for anyone $$ you shouldn't
do anything unless it's for yourself $$ katharine is a self-
made kind of woman $$ mami is too $$ katharine comes
to the house & mami waxes her in the living room $$ she
makes me set up the dining room table into a waxing bed
$$ the same one we eat our twisted thanksgiving on $$
arroz con gandules even tho we aren't puerto rican $$ sweet
potato casserole recipe mami got from one of her clients $$
katharine comes on time $$ she has no tolerance for people
being late $$ i am reading in the kitchen but eavesdropping
$$ immigrant kids know how to listen $$ it is how we get
ahead $$ we are good little spies $$ katharine says have you
heard about this george zimmerman thing? $$ mami says
no, what is about? $$ katharine says well everyone wants to
make it a race thing but it isn't a race thing because george
zimmerman is *latino* $$ mami says okay lift up your legs $$
mami says to be honest, i don't really get it $$ katharine says
i just don't know why people have to be politically correct
about it $$ later, katharine will play devil's advocate with
morals on facebook, later still, she will say we are all immi-

grants, aren't we $$ now she says i mean you came here & worked so hard i just really admire that $$ mami calls my name $$ meleessa please heat up de wax $$ oh, katharine says, your daughter, i haven't seen her in ages $$ is she still reading? she is so well behaved $$ you did such a good job with them $$ you always do such a good job.

Melissa Lozada-Oliva is the author of the chapbooks *Plastic Pajaros, Rude Girl is Lonely Girl!* (Pizza Pi Press), and *Peluda* (Button Poetry, 2017), which investigates the intersecting narratives of body image, hair-removal, and Latina identity. Her works have been featured in *The Guardian, Huffington Post, REMEZCLA, Muzzle Magazine,* and her mom's Facebook statuses. She is a VONA alumnae and currently an MFA candidate at New York University.

Justin Herrmann :
Acts of Love

[From *Tahoma Literary Review*, Issue 10, Summer 2017]

It's 10 am, our first weekend away from our baby. Flora drains her bottle, and then sips my flat, sour tap beer.

"Bad tap lines," she says.

"Hard to say. That taste might be a feature of the beer," I say.

"Gym socks isn't a feature any brewer goes after." She slaps her thin hand against the black Formica bar top. "Patrick Swayze," she says, "there's something wrong with your taps. Give us bottles of Bud and shots of Jim." The bartender does look like a young Patrick Swayze; a leotard-tight shirt displays each curve of his lean muscles. Make no mistake though, this place isn't *Road House*. Racks of Edgar Allan Poe merchandise line one of the walls.

"Two things I never question," Swayze says, "a beautiful woman's sense of taste and their opinions on footwear." He pops the Budweiser caps.

I hold up my hand. "I'll finish my beer," I say. It's awful. I say to Flora, "That tasted like all the meals my grandmother fed me."

"Can't shoplift McDonald's nuggets," she says.

I was arrested the first time at age nine for stealing toothbrushes with my grandmother. Truck-driving dad, mother too many complications to list, Flora knows my story.

"She made sacrifices," I say.

"I don't know anything about sacrifices," she says, then drinks deeply from her bottle. I know her story too, and I know she gets like this when she drinks, in a donating-blood-wouldn't-mean-a-thing-if-it-wasn't-pumped-into-her-veins kind of mood.

"Sweetheart," I say, "if I knew you when I shoplifted, I'd have stuffed long-stem roses down the front of my pants for you."

Her eyes brighten like torches. She nods towards the Poe merchandise and mouths, "Show me."

I know I shouldn't, but I'm encouraged by my hatred of young Swayze's flowing hair, judgmentally waving in the stale breeze of the overhead ventilation unit. I drink my shot, then her shot.

On the way back from the toilets, I stop at the merchandise, finger shirt material, flip through a poetry collection. I turn back to recite a stanza of "Annabel Lee," but Swayze is pouring shots. Him and Flora clink glasses and drink. I move behind the rotating postcard rack. They giggle. He asks her something. She touches his hand.

One postcard reads, *Never to suffer would never to have been blessed.* It has a picture of Poe's dismal face. He looks like a mustached Peyton Manning, someone else who's contributed to my suffering over the years.

Swayze hands Flora a pen. She writes something on a cocktail napkin, brings the napkin to her mouth, and then hands it to Swayze.

He places it in his back pocket. I knew about things in the early days between us. Once I found greasy yeti-sized hand prints on the kitchen table, countertops, even reflecting from glossy pear skins in the fruit basket. I couldn't eat at home for weeks. After she got pregnant, things changed, felt domestic. She learned to use oil for cooking.

I find a postcard that reads, *I was never really insane except upon occasions when my heart was touched*. I slip it into my back pocket. While I'm at it I pocket a deck of playing cards full of depressed-looking ravens, and a small flask that's simply engraved *Never More*.

Swayze holds Flora's arm, examines the snake-scale tattoos from her knuckles to her shoulder. I walk to the bar and take Flora's wrist from Swayze. I make a production of kissing all the way up her bare arm.

"This is a special occasion," I say. "Frozen margaritas for my true love and me."

Swayze turns and digs the blender from underneath the opposite counter. I release Flora's beautiful wrist and lean over the bar, channel a delicate touch I haven't needed since my petty crime days. I grip the note poking from the impractical pocket of his bikini-tight pants. I unfold it, smooth the creases with both hands, then slam it against the bar.

Flora looks at the note, then looks to see if there's anything she hasn't yet consumed. She takes a bottle, drinks the last sad drops. Swayze places the blender on the bar, smooths his hair.

Flora's mouth is open and beautiful and dumb, as if each impact the chambers of her heart make speak for themselves. She reaches into her large purse, pulls out a smaller purse, and then pulls out the smallest purse that holds her cash. She unfolds a few twenties.

"This should cover everything including the shit in his pockets," she says to Swayze.

I run my hand over the napkin, squint to read Flora's awful, unmistakable scrawl. On the napkin is a ten-digit phone number that does not belong to her, nor does the name with nipples drawn on the double O's belong to her.

There is something new about the look in Flora's eyes, as is the way her face contorts as the tears begin. Between gasps and sobs she says, "I want my baby."

I take Flora's hand. She resists, and then leads me towards the door.

"Thanks for visiting the Dreary Raven. We're sorry we're open," Swayze says as we step into sunlight, leaning into each other, both a little unsteady.

Justin Herrmann is the author of the story collection *Highway One, Antarctica* (MadHat Press, 2014). He's a *River Styx* Microfiction Contest winner and his stories have appeared in journals including *Crab Orchard Review*, *SmokeLong Quarterly*, *The Tishman Review*, and *BULL: Men's Fiction*. He has an MFA from University of Alaska Anchorage, and spent 24 months living and working with good people at McMurdo Station, Antarctica. Come drink a beer with him next time you're in Kotzebue, Alaska.

Monet Patrice Thomas :
Ring of Salt

[From *(b)OINK*, Issue 7, August 2017]

Because she was curious, she'd let him pull down her jeans. They were twenty-one. His fingers dug into her hips as he worked the material from side to side, a smooth technique she noted from somewhere behind a vodka fog. The way his mouth followed every place his hands touched was a skill she would not have assigned to him, even though he was her oldest friend. Since middle school, she'd known all of his girlfriends, was hated by them all. One had attempted to include her in a threesome, a move to entice him, an act of desperation. But in declining, she'd made that girl the biggest enemy of them all. Because she'd known him for so long she was a threat. She'd known what he was scared of, what he dreamed of, who he'd wanted to be, but sex, well, that was kept safe inside a ring of salt.

It had been cold down in his parents' basement. And when she'd let her head fall back to rest on the top of the musty old couch, she could see snow piling up against the only window in the room. Little hairs raised with a shiver on her upper thighs bringing with them a moment of fleeting doubt. If he had been another man she would've been embarrassed she hadn't shaved. Instead she'd felt as unconcerned as if she'd been standing in a women's locker room, and maybe, that wasn't the way a woman should feel about a man with his head where it was below her waist. Then the pants were gone completely and he was murmuring to the sensitive flesh behind her knees. "Relax." Then she was warm, everywhere.

She'll never forget the self-assured way he brought her to orgasm—not the next day, not the next holiday when she was back in town, but didn't call him. And not the following year when she saw him just across the street, but didn't call out. She'll never forget the silken texture of his hair between her fingers as she pressed herself to his mouth. She'll never forget how he made a sound, an almost growl, when she was close, and how it had brought forth a companion sound in her own throat. She'll never forget the way he looked when she finally opened her eyes: his chest rising and falling, lips swollen, and hair wrecked and regarding her the way he always had—across rooms and tables—like she was the world.

Monet Patrice Thomas is a black poet and writer from North Carolina. She has an MFA in poetry from the Inland Northwest Center for Writers at Eastern Washington University in Spokane, Washington. In 2016 she attended the Tin House Summer Workshop for a nonfiction workshop under the guidance of Kiese Laymon. This is her second year as a reader for The *Wigleaf* Top 50 and her first year conducting interviews for *The Rumpus*. monetpatricethomas.com

Rumaan Alam :
Minuet

[From *Wigleaf*, April 27, 2017]

I knew this guy, such a nice guy, a barrage of jokes and *drinks-on-me*, who was once married to a girl—we were all friends, the three of us—who I liked quite a bit even if I never truly knew her, but does anyone ever know anyone, and they divorced after a year or two, I can't remember, anyway it wasn't a surprise because I knew them both and liked them both but thought them ill-matched and even though you never know what goes on inside a marriage, you can guess, and I guessed correctly and the divorce was hard as divorces are but the thing is she threw herself into her work and so did he, and they separately became quite successful, though how do you measure success really, well they made some money and were good people to boot so that's success right?

Anyway she met someone and so did he, and I guess it's no surprise that she met this other man at work and he this other woman at work, because honestly, how does anyone in this society know anyone else, I have no idea how I would contrive to meet someone outside a professional context, anyway she met this guy who is handsome and tall and curious about the world and he met this woman who is lovely and curvaceous and has a big sarcastic laugh, and in this one very real sense it's a happy end, or it's like one of those old ballroom dances, maybe a minuet is what I mean, where you begin with one person but end with another person and somehow it's all in fun and you get to listen to J.S. Bach.

Then it happens I ran into him, mister jokes, mister good times, on the bus, when I was on my way home from work and he was on his way to a restaurant to meet his new wife, well, she's not new, anymore, but his wife, and he hugged me warmly and I said how are you and he told me that his wife was pregnant but what he said was We're pregnant even though we all know that's a solo activity, and I said congratulations and squeezed his bicep and it was that way that it is when you see an old friend, someone you knew years ago, by which I mean it wasn't me in bifocals or him with little lines by the sides of his mouth but it was our selves at twenty which were perfect in this way that we took quite for granted which is I guess what people mean about youth being wasted on the young, our healthy, strong bodies, which we abused by drinking terrible beer and wandering around until three in the morning then eating scrambled eggs.

Since we were old friends catching up on the bus, I said, oh I saw your ex-wife, because it amused me, you know, to be thirty-seven, on a bus, talking about someone's ex-wife, to use the noun ex-wife, it felt so adult in this delicious way like when you spend eighty dollars on a bottle of wine because you're an adult and you can and he said how is she and I said well, she's ok, but I was not telling the truth because she was not good, or was but there was a sadness there because it turned out her new guy not only didn't want to marry her he didn't want to have children and she was a thirty-eight year old woman and she kind of wanted that stuff and was reckoning, I guess, with the fact that the life she had made for herself wouldn't after all contain what she'd thought it might when she was a little girl and even though I still don't know her well she just confessed all this stuff to me so it must have been weighing on her.

And the bus kind of rounded this corner so our bodies shifted because of some law of physics and his chest kind of pressed into mine and it was like we were going to kiss or something just for a minute but we're of a generation of men that's at ease with that kind of intimacy or proximity between men, like we don't need to couch it in football, we don't need sports as an excuse to touch one another, because a body needs to be touched and my friend was going to meet his pregnant wife and there I was with news of his ex-wife who we both knew would never be pregnant because that window closes, eventually, as windows do, and suddenly this reunion seemed sad or something, and I had this feeling that I wouldn't see this old friend or his ex-wife for a long time or maybe ever again and in that moment, it was like I was inside his mind, and I knew he was remembering an affection for that first wife that he had maybe forgotten until I brought up her name, and I saw the joy of the fact that he had a new wife, a new life, and soon, a new baby, I saw that joy disappear, I saw that something changed, a little light went out in his eyes, because he realized in that moment we can't touch someone's body, someone's life, without affecting it, and there's no going back in time, and you never stop loving or feeling, really, and then it was time for me to get off the bus and I walked home and took a hot shower.

Rumaan Alam is the author of the novels *Rich and Pretty* (Ecco, 2016) and *That Kind of Mother* (HarperCollins, 2018). His writing has appeared in the *New York Times*, *Elle*, *New York Magazine*, the *Wall Street Journal*, *Buzzfeed*, and elsewhere. He studied at Oberlin College, and now lives in New York.

Denise Tolan :
Because You are Dead

[From *Lunch Ticket*, Amuse-Bouche, June 2017]

You don't know I have a picture of you, because you are dead.

Before you were dead, I wondered what it would be like to be trapped in your mouth for eternity, like a wedded Jonah. Whenever you said honey or Leeza or, more likely, Lisa, I would feel the rib cage constrict.

I have some regrets from before you died.

Once you wanted a burger from Sonic. You were working and I was not, so I went to get one for you.

Pickles, onions, cheese, but no mustard, you said.

Pickles, onions, cheese, but no mustard, I repeated into the speaker.

When I handed you the burger you opened it, then looked at me as if I'd broken your crayon.

Mustard, you said, pointing to the offending yellow.

I stood in front of you, wondering what had gone wrong.

I wish I'd done a better job with the burger order but only because, somehow, you are dead.

Once, after a late dinner with your coworkers, we sat in your car while you decided what to do. You were tired, but there was a possibility of sex in the air; distant, like the sound of wind or waves.

Tell me a fantasy, you finally said.

Tell you a fantasy, I repeated as a question, as if I was giving it thought.

I needed sleep too, but I told you what you wanted to hear—the girl who lived downstairs from me—you, sticky with new moisture—three mouths, taking in, spilling out.

I'd unbuttoned my shirt and lazily played with one nipple as I spoke.

Let's go inside, you said. I knocked on her door as we passed by.

I wonder if, for the dead, that makes up for the mustard.

You held out your hand once revealing a single green disk the size of a tear.

Beach glass? I asked.

You brought the glass closer to my face, as if it might be some kind of ancient tell, like when children hold butter-cups to their throats as a predictor of their affinity for butter.

You saw me in that glass, beautiful and valuable and different. I wanted to believe you were not wrong.

It was me. Is me.

But in the end it was common glass. Washed ashore. Held in the mouth of the sea until it was spit out, edges smoothed by the force of its current disdain.

The dead, most likely, let go of regret and beach glass.

The picture you don't know I have is from your obituary. Before you were dead someone you loved must have taken it because you forgot to guard your eyes when you looked into the lens. The photograph is in sepia, which makes so much sense, since you were always the color of an ancient map; never really accurate, but promising adventure nonetheless.

Denise Tolan's stories and essays have appeared in *Lunch Ticket*, *Hobart*, *The Saturday Evening Post*, *Apple Valley Review*, *The Tishman Review*, and others. Her work was named in *Wigleaf*'s Top 50 and included in The Best Short Stories from *The Saturday Evening Post* Fiction Contest 2017. Denise is a graduate of the Red Earth MFA in Creative Writing Program at Oklahoma City University. She is shopping a collection of short fiction, *Weighting*, and is currently completing a novel, *Tales the Fat Chick Told*. You can find more information about her obsession with Moby-Dick at dtolan4723.wixsite.com/denisetolan.

Allegra Hyde :
Lowry Hill

[From *The Adroit Journal*, Issue 19, Jan. 2017]

The neighborhood was filled with big girthy houses, toad-like, squatting on plots of land—on a low hill overlooking the city—houses three stories tall and girdled by screened-in porches, open-air decks, houses set down on the earth like fists.

It was spring. The air whizzed with rain-hail, stinging our faces, and later smudged white with snow—winter's last gasp—but the snow was cottony and infirm, and had melted by noon our second day when the weather lifted and the sun became brave, buttery, and it was as if there had never been a winter at all.

This we watched with cautious hope, like the survivors of a wreck. The neighborhood was not our neighborhood—nor even in our city—and likely never would be, but we felt this spring was our spring also. We felt ourselves stripped and squeezed by the shifting seasons, our bodies caught in cosmic gears, like rodents in a clock.

"We should live here," one of my friends said, trying to sound ambiguous. We were always trying to sound ambiguous. We were artists—or we wanted to be—which seemed reason enough to cultivate a coyness about our intentions.

We cultivated other things, too. Transiency. Radicalism. Poor posture. Debt.

But it was difficult to stem the desire in our words: this place, this little neighborhood, had gripped our sheltered hearts.

It was spring and the trees were sticklings, dead-looking, flagged by the dry-brown husks of last year's leaves, except for the places where new buds pressed forth, tight and green-tipped, live as grenades. The trees quivered even when there wasn't any wind, as did the hedgerows—bare-boned and see-through—the scheming forsythia, all things anticipating their own chaos.

We anticipated our own chaos.

We walked in circles around and around the neighborhood, hallucinating surrender.

We too held our breath.

Travel is a dream state, a chimera, even when done for mundane reasons, even when reasoned with mundane rationale. We were young and wanted new places to love us. And, truly, we saw ourselves mirrored in puddles: our dark hats and our upturned collars and our smoke-singed eyes. We saw ourselves in the windows of those big houses on that low hill overlooking the city: our dark hats and our upturned collars and our smoke-singed eyes watching someone else's spring.

"We should live here," my friend said again, this time without the inflection.

We became sour-mouthed with longing. Our knuckles ached. To travel is to believe you've left everything behind, including your delusions. To travel is to believe that by moving through time and space you are making some kind of progress.

Those fat houses, built with brick and trimmed by black shutters, or else wooden and painted white, columns Corinthian, moldings ornate as cake piping; houses windowed with stained glass, TVs winking kaleidoscopic; houses announced by wind chimes, the moan of microwaves and, later, by chicken-brothy smells; houses sentineled by three-foot basketball hoops, by three-foot hounds; houses with porches bloating onto lawns scrubbed raw and restless. And flowerbeds—dirt dark, wet—casting passing soles in ripe brown plaster. They too trembled as the green claws of daffodils and tulips knifed upwards, so new their color tingled, neon and frantic. If you watch long enough you can see them move. If you watch long enough you believe they are watching you. If you watch long enough you believe they won't break your heart.

Allegra Hyde's debut story collection, *Of This New World* (University of Iowa Press, 2016), won the John Simmons Short Fiction Award. Her stories and essays have been published by *Tin House*, *Kenyon Review*, *New England Review*, and other venues. She is the recipient of two Pushcart Prizes, as well as support from The Elizabeth George Foundation, the Lucas Artist Residency Program, the Jentel Foundation, the Bread Loaf Writers' Conference, and the U.S. Fulbright Commission. allegrahyde.com

Alex McElroy :
A Man and a Man

[From *Daddy Issues*, The Cupboard Pamphlet, Vol. 30, 2017. The story originally appeared in *The Adroit Journal*]

A man and a man went to a bar. One man was a celebrity; the other was sad. The celebrity was alarmingly handsome and witty; the sad man was a nurse, a nurturing man, who tried to see the goodness of life. They went to the bar to pretend they were friends. As boys, they had been friends. They jumped off roofs and set dead squirrels ablaze. But as adults they preferred to pretend.

At the bar, they drank Cutty Sark and remembered out loud. They shared with each other their secrets. The sad man's secrets were boring. This wasn't his fault. Celebrity secrets are superior to the secrets of everyday folks. They receive fresh secrets every day from an app on their phones, marvelous secrets, secrets too secret for everyday folks, the folks who pay taxes and fart and sneak little cookies at night. These secrets were not meant to be spread beyond the realm of celebrities, but the celebrity pitied his friend, so he opened his app and said, "America will run out of water by 2019."

"But I wanted a family," said the sad man. He decided to hide what he'd learned from his wife.

"Ha, ha!" laughed the celebrity. "Look at your face!" He smiled a beam of light.

The sad man knew he'd been had and tried to conceal his displeasure. He was a small, gullible man, loving and shy, who knew too well what it was like to be played for a fool. His short temper had made him a prime target when he was a child. Children love making children incensed. And the sad man, feeling once again like the target of malevolent children, he reacted brashly. The Cutty Sark had heated his head, melting away the restraints in his brain. He said, "Remember when you were in love with my wife?"

"I am still in love with your wife," the celebrity said. "She is why I became a celebrity. Women cannot resist a celebrity."

This was not the response the sad man had expected or wanted. Flustered, he ran to the bathroom, where he sat in the stall reading texts from his wife—*kasha and 2% milk*; *let's rent a movie tomorrow*; *when is the dentist?*—and recalled the love letters he'd written to her before they were married. The letters were intense, passionate pleas in which he promised to treat her how she deserved to be treated. She was dating the celebrity then—when he was just an anxious young man with comical goals—and the sad man told her she deserved more than a selfish, wannabe actor. The sad man had an enormous heart. He emptied the juice of his heart into every letter he wrote. His unadulterated affection had attracted his wife, he reminded himself, boosting his ego as he returned to the bar.

The celebrity had ordered another round.

Cautiously, the sad man took a sip.

"Dee-dee," said the celebrity. *Dee-dee* was the sad man's nickname. Celebrities loved using nicknames. "Dee-dee, I've got something that I need to tell you."

A sense of foreboding enveloped the sad man. He wanted to be with his wife.

The celebrity said, "I don't know how to say this so I'm just gonna say it, Dee-dee, because that's how I am: a straight shooter, givin' it straight, it's the best I can do for us both because you deserve it, you're a good goddamn man, my best-best friend in the whole wide world, so here it is. Dee-dee, your wife is ten thousand birds."

"Ten thousand birds?"

"You heard that right, Dee-dee. Ten-Kay, a smattering of sparrows."

"My wife is not ten thousand birds."

"It's unbelievable, right? I never believed it myself. But it's true, Dee-dee, and she's kept it from you for reasons I don't understand."

"You're unbelievable. You're insane." The sad man had heard of men like the men being described. Men who had come home after business trips, weekends out—hell, trips to the gym—to find in place of their wives caterpillars wiggling, or a pod of seals, flopping and slapping their fins on the carpet. But birds? Ten thousand birds? "I'm not gonna fall for your trick," the sad man said.

The celebrity promised it wasn't a trick.

"She's my wife. She married me, and you're—"

"I'm jealous, yes, because, Dee-dee, you stole her away from me. But me, I've got nothing to worry about. Someday soon she'll walk out on you. Know why?"

"Oh please, please tell me why my wife's gonna leave."

"Because your wife is ten thousand birds. And ten thousand birds, they cannot be caged."

The sad man waved off the celebrity. He left the bar and started walking toward home. The air was thick and moist, like that of a bathroom after a shower. The celebrity's words had tugged him inside out. He studied his memories. How did his wife normally speak? Chirpy and high? Her head, how did she shift her neck? Quickly? With erratic simplicity? The sad man's hands trembled. His legs felt rubbered. He feared what he might find, or what he wouldn't find, but see nevertheless, when he talked to his wife.

She was not on the couch. She was not in the kitchen. He heard her inside their bedroom. He put his ear to the door and sank to his knees, listening to the sound of her flapping, the rustle of wind fluttering papers and sheets, the patter of ten thousand miniature hearts relentlessly beating. He opened the door. The bedroom was empty.

Alex McElroy's writing appears in *The Atlantic*, *Tin House*, *The Kenyon Review Online*, *TriQuarterly*, *New England Review*, *Conjunctions*, and elsewhere. His chapbook, *Daddy Issues*, won the 2016 Editors' Prize from *The Cupboard Pamphlet*, and he is the recipient of the 2018 Inprint Donald Barthelme Prize for Nonfiction. He has received fellowships from the Virginia G. Piper Center, The Elizabeth George Foundation, and The National Parks Service. Currently, he is a print fiction editor for *Gulf Coast*.

Amanda O'Callaghan :
Tying the Boats

[From *bathflashfictionaward.com*, June 2017 and in *The Lobsters Run Free*, Bath Flash Fiction Award anthology Vol. 2, December 2017]

A week after she married him, she cut her hair. The scissors made a hungry sound working their way through the curls.

"You cut your hair," he said, when he came home. Nothing more.

She thought he might have said, "You cut off your beautiful hair," but his mouth could not make the shape of beautiful, even then.

She kept the hair in a drawer. A great hank of it, bound together in two places with ribbon almost the same dark red. Sometimes, when she was searching in the big oak chest that she brought from home, she'd see it stretched against the back of the drawer, flattened into the joinery like a sleek, cowering animal.

Once, she lifted it out, held it up to the light to catch the last of its fading lustre. She weighed it in her hands. The hair was thick, substantial, heavy as the ropes they'd used when she was a girl, tying the boats when storms were coming.

Amanda O'Callaghan

Amanda O'Callaghan's short stories and flash fiction have been published and won awards in Australia, UK, and Ireland. A former advertising executive, she has a BA and MA in English from King's College, London. She holds a PhD in English from the University of Queensland. Amanda has won the Bath Flash Fiction Award, Flash 500, the Aeon Award, and the Carmel Bird Award. She was a finalist in the 2017 Bristol Short Story Prize. She lives in Brisbane, Australia, where she is completing her first collection of stories. amandaocallaghan.com

Eric Blix :

Triptych

[From *The Collagist*, Issue 93, (October 15) 2017]

A Disturbance

"It was likely the single most important thing ever to happen to Protagonist. Walking home from school, back when children were allowed to do such a thing, back before pedophilic monsters roamed the streets, Protagonist would camp in a handmade fort behind the local hardware store until dark set in. I think it was mostly empty crates and probably some rotting cardboard. I'm not sure. Protagonist is not very forthcoming about this period. The kids at school were nasty creatures. I know that much. One day, Protagonist was in the fort eating animal crackers when a bomb rolled into the alley. The bomb exploded, and Protagonist's body was blown apart. They found limbs and viscera for several thousand feet in all directions. That stupid kid never listened to me. 'Duck and cover,' I'd say, but that stupid kid would never listen."

Duck and Cover

A choreography that places the body in unanticipated communication with itself. A whole movement of ballon, in which the dancers float and sink alternatingly on the front and back beats. Next comes the idle hour, after the low notes have dropped, in which the strongest female dancer in the company stands arabesque for as long as she can endure at the front of the stage. The artistry of the posture is involuntary. Held for such lengths, her pose engages the minor muscles and runs them to excruciating ends. Her body eventually comes to a complete and uninterrupted tremor. She seems as if she will rupture. The noted 1983 performance given by the Moscow State Academy of Choreography at the Bolshoi Theater: in which Nina Ananiashvili balanced on her right foot for two entire hours. Her screams of pain grew and eventually merged with the low, off-key drone of the accompanying sousaphone, such that one sound could not be separated from the other. Protagonist was amazed. It seemed as if such a thing had never happened before.

Such a Thing had Never Happened Before

Three men brought to this exact house by the guiding light of a star. They trekked forward, hungry from their travels, convinced the star had been placed for them by God. They traveled for thirty days, and the star never so much as flickered. They came to see Protagonist, who accepted their gifts of gold and local grains and spices. "Did you ever see that picture?" Protagonist said to the eldest, after dinner. "Did you ever see that picture where the Germans drove their tanks straight into the East Siberian Sea?" No, the eldest had not seen it. "I was hoping you remembered what it was called."

"How is your daughter?"

"Daughter?"

"Yes, the one with the child."

Protagonist lifted a bowl of grains and smelled.

"Your daughter had a child, you know. That's why we're here."

"Is it, now?"

Later, after the men had left, Protagonist followed their footprints. They never did find a body. Only a pair of shoes—only a disturbance in the snow.

Eric Blix is the author of the short story collection, *Physically Alarming Men* (Stephen F. Austin State University Press, 2017). His writing has appeared in such journals as *Caketrain*, *The Pinch*, *Western Humanities Review*, and others. Born and raised in Minnesota, he earned his MFA at Minnesota State University, Mankato. Currently, he lives in Salt Lake City, where he studies in the PhD program in Literature and Creative Writing at the University of Utah.

Quinn Madison :
Crickets

[From *(b)OINK*, Summer 2017]

Mornings, the shouts of my landlady rise through the floor-boards as she rails against her husband. In bed, I press wet tea leaves against my eyelids. I moved to Taiwan without a plan.

Midnights I mount Li Kai's motorcycle, press my cheek hard against his back, circle my arms tightly around his waist. If I could, I'd wrap my legs around him, erase the air between us.

Snake Alley calls. There, we perch on wooden stools in the street, drink shots of snake whiskey so fast our eyesight blurs. We see girls leaning out from barred windows of tilted shacks, waving delicate hands to men hungry for something dark beyond description.

Tonight the youngest girl is pushed forward. Each man, each trembling weed, wants to wrap himself around her doll waist, arch her back, enter her in measured thrusts. I know she dreads morning, the coarseness of the bamboo mat, the serpent breath that'll cling to her. I know she believes only in her nightmares.

* * *

Always, when night ends an invisible border shifts.

I talk with my landlady mornings before my Mandarin class. Once, while cracking sunflower seeds between her teeth, she tells me that her mother arranged her marriage. "Ta bu hao kan," she says.

She spits a shell, repeats that her husband of twenty years is ugly. She pushes him away most nights, recoils at his sweat of ash and alcohol, his cheap whispered dreams of wealth. In this city of pagodas and glass spiral towers, of blackened air and exhausted trees, she feels despair. She knows her future is already here: winters of dumplings dropped in hot peanut oil, the coming and going of her soldier sons, the livid heat of summers. Hoping heaven will reveal its intentions, she searches the night sky for messages—a flicker on the fire planet perhaps.

Anything.

After so many lives, she's tired. She hoards rent in a worn silk pouch and breeds crickets for extra cash. For weeks now she has heard something no one else does: a ringing. She tilts her head to shake it out, claps hands against her head.

Now her finger floats towards me, then points to her ear. I rest my hand on her shoulder, peer into the dark cavity. I look for something, a movement perhaps, an injury.

I tell her I see only blackness. She scolds me, commands me to her again. I press my ear to hers, listen. Suddenly, sounds. They rise through her body like birds, enter me like wind. I hear her life, the wet clothes flapping against acres of line, the screech of caged crickets, the chop chop chop of her kitchen knife against the cutting board.

She takes a step back, looks at me with uncertainty. I want to soothe her. She should know there's no beginning or end to our revisions. That we can live in greens and blues radiant with revelation. That we don't have to be tamed. That love can silence our whispering ghosts.

Quinn Madison

Quinn Madison has a master's degree in social anthropology from Oxford University, which means she's a practiced people-watcher. She spent a year in Taipei on a Sachar Fellowship, researching the lives of contemporary women fiction writers. Her story "Anhui" was nominated by *Zyzzyva* for a Pushcart Prize. She works weekdays as a content strategist in San Francisco and writes fiction in Oakland cafes on weekends.

Denise Howard Long :
What We See

[From *The Tishman Review*, Vol. Three, Issue One: January 2017]

The baby began walking just a few months after being born, proving she was as exceptional as we had planned for her to be. But she refused to walk during the day. Only at night. When we were asleep.

At first I wasn't certain what was going on; I only knew that in the morning something felt different. A shift as subtle as the temperature dropping mildly or the wind slightly shifting its direction. A feeling that, in some ways, only a mother would know.

But, in time, my husband sensed it too. Then he'd ask if I was feeling all right, ask if I also felt something was off, some indescribable thing different from before.

Before what, I had asked, still trying to piece it together myself. He'd shrug and assure me it was probably nothing.

And we'd check on our sleeping baby before he'd scuttle off to work.

There she was, asleep in her crib, pacifier tucked between her lips. Always her arms flung out from her sides, as if she'd fallen to the mattress from a great height. But as I laid my hand upon her chest, feeling the rise and fall of her breaths,

I noticed the blackened bottoms of her footie pajamas. I knew without a doubt she'd been up to something.

And then there were the more obvious traces she began to leave behind.

Dishes my husband had left on the counter were now washed and put away. But they were in the cabinets upside down, stacked in precarious sculptures poised to fall when I opened the door.

My toothbrush would be pulled from its cup, resting on the counter, sticky globs of pale blue toothpaste clinging to the bristles and dripping down the side—one more thing for me to scrub.

At first, my husband laughed and thought I was joking. But I showed him the pajamas, the dishes, reminded him of the morning air that had felt different for days. I thought he would laugh, tell me I was crazy, but he didn't. He thought it was cute. These little things that would happen while we slept. He marveled at her cleverness and ingenuity and told me *that's our girl*.

I'd smiled and agreed that *yes, she most certainly was*.

One morning the garage door was left open, the engine running in one of the cars, my husband swearing he hadn't left the keys in the ignition this time.

The baby still refused to walk during the day. She was sitting up easily now.

Sometimes she would stand, gurgles of baby drool clinging to her lips. But in that moment we were prepared for her to move, she'd collapse, her ripe diaper hitting the carpet like soured fruit.

I'd watch my husband to see if he noticed her smirk like I had. And he'd sigh and ask me again what she and I did all day, and I wondered again what I was missing that I should somehow see.

He thought if we could make the baby stop walking at night she'd have to walk in the day. Then we could record videos of her toddling, one foot in front of the other, and post them online for the entire world to see, sharing her in a way we'd avoided because our secret was too strange to believe.

The first attempt was putting the baby gate across her bedroom door at night. But in the morning, the gate was folded neatly in the hall.

We tried staying up all night, waiting. But my husband could never stay awake during his turn to watch.

We set up a camera in her room to catch her in the act but no matter how we placed it, the angle was never quite right.

Each night, we'd creep into her room on our way to bed and we'd watch her sleep. Lingering, I'd become lost in the idea that I was there, standing right on the lavender rug that I'd selected over a year earlier, and she had no idea.

The air in our house became stifling: a dense, warm sensation filling us both with the unknown. I could see it in my husband's eyes, the fear of what we needed to witness but couldn't figure out how. A feeling of unease grew deep in my body, my feet always heavy.

I mentioned perhaps putting a lock on her door, from the outside, the idea giving way in my mind like rocks knocked loose by rushing water.

But what about a fire? my husband said. *She wouldn't be able to get out.*

Later, he would deny it had been his idea.

What we both agreed to was intended to be a small kitchen fire. A few splashes of gasoline and the flick of a match. Just enough that the baby would smell the smoke and walk out. And we'd see her. We'd see her coming outside, walking, and it would be night but we would see.

And as we stood on the lawn, watching the flames climb higher and higher, my husband pulled away, moved toward the house. And I dug my nails into his arm and said, *Wait. Just a little bit more. I still want to see.*

Denise Howard Long is the author of the flash fiction chapbook *Spoil the Child* (Finishing Line Press, 2018) and her fiction has appeared in *[PANK]*, *SmokeLong Quarterly*, *Pithead Chapel*, *Evansville Review*, *Blue Monday Review*, and elsewhere. Her story "Recuerdos Olvidados" was runner-up for the Larry Brown Short Story Award, and her story "Where It's Buried" won *Five on the Fifth*'s Annual Short Story Contest. She has been awarded residencies from Hedgebrook and Dorland Mountain Arts Colony. Originally from Illinois, Denise currently lives in Nebraska, with her husband and two sons, where she is working on a novel. denisehlong.com

Meg Pokrass :
Barista

[From *The Del Sol Review*, September 2017]

That night, it was just me and the barista. Everyone else was finally gone. He was standing in the middle of the social area, waiting for the world to quiet down so he could serve me properly. I stood right next to him at his invisible espresso bar, holding his hand in the wilting light.

Earlier, I was worried about the teenager. I heard her on the phone with her mother. "No, no, no! You aren't hearing me! I'm not staying here over fucking, fucking Christmas!"

And then she cried. Christmas had most of us all by the neck. She slammed her not-smart phone onto the floor, a sad little crazy thing, so I asked her if she wanted a cup of something. "Espresso," she said.

"A shot for the young lady," I said to the barista. In a way, she belonged to all of us.

He looked like a confused nurse, as if it was time for treatment, but he'd forgotten who to treat. "Tell your family that it wasn't so bad here?" he said.

Somehow, the barista heard that one of us was going to be released. "Must be you," he said. This was right, I was scheduled, but I wasn't sure that I wanted out.

"Tell them about the drinks I made you."

"Promise," I said.

Holiday cards were being taped to the wall near the TV by a nurse I had never seen before.

"I have to die here for everyone," he said. He said this every day. I had gotten used to him saying it.

I looked at the teenager. She sat on the floor, her arms protecting herself. Soon, she'd walk around the social area asking everyone if they found her to be physically beautiful. Each and every one of us would tell her that we did.

Meg Pokrass is the author of four collections of flash fiction and one award-winning collection of prose poetry, *Cellulose Pajamas*, which received the Blue Light Book Award in 2016. Her flash fiction has been widely anthologized in two Norton Anthologies: *Flash Fiction International* and *New Micro-Exceptionally Short Fiction*. A new flash fiction collection, *Alligators At Night* will be released in 2018. She is the founder of *New Flash Fiction Review* and co-founder of San Francisco's Flash Fiction Collective reading series. She teaches flash fiction workshops and serves as Festival Curator for the Flash Fiction Festival, UK.

Hala Alyan :
Armadillo

[From *great weather for MEDIA*, The Other Side of
Violet, 2017]

I know there was a boat. My mother, seventeen, her hair
tangled in the sea breeze. She is sitting near the rudder.
There is my father: mustached, cigarette-lipped, answering
prime minister when anyone asked what he'd do with his
life. Kuwait, early 1980s, and the world was as pretty as it had
ever been.

~~~~

These things happen. My father said I love you; my mother
kept the baby. Like a lighthouse during a Nor'easter, theirs
was a love filled with static. Impossible to decipher. *You're all
I ever* became *I wish I'd never.*

~~~~

The children are three little houses. One built with wind,
one with grass, the third with brick. The windows aren't
windows at all.

~~~~

Once, we went to New Orleans for vacation. We slunk through the swamp and everyone saw an armadillo except my brother. He cried for it to re-emerge. A family joke ever since.

Years later, my brother became afraid on a rollercoaster and my father yelled at the operator—some Kansas kid—to make it stop. He did.

Sometimes, I tell my brother, *I wonder if I ever saw the armadillo myself.*

~~~~

My mother is sitting in the basement of our Maine house. There is a blizzard and I've just learnt the word for shelter in French. She is pregnant, and crying.

~~~~

Vierzon, three hours south of Paris. We are all lying in the dark, watching the old stars with their owl-eyes. We are predicting our horoscopes for the coming years. None of it comes true. I marry. Talal stops drinking. Miriam gets older. The Doha villa still makes me cry and it takes a decade to understand what my parents always knew: all the love in the world won't buy you what you wanted in the first place.

~~~~

When Hezbollah captured those Israeli soldiers, my parents argued with guests, aunts and uncles, neighbors. They were two hearts of the same machine. They shut every room up.

I'm fickle, yes, but every klepto is a romantic at heart. I circled entire houses just to watch my mother's cheek on my father's shoulder. Each was the fever the other learned to live with.

When my mother returned from Scotland with her graduation robe, my father rushed to the door murmuring *my doctor, my doctor.*

Don't tell me that it isn't love. You haven't seen the photographs. Their small, young faces. My mother wore layers of white lace. My father clapped while the guests danced.

~~~~

What do we do with heartache? Tow it.

~~~~

I know there was a boat. Before my father slammed a car door and walked across a Midwestern highway. Before the Portland fight where my mother dropped a plate of lobster. Before *did you hear him say habibti,* my brother and I nudging each other at every kiss, this whole goddamn world the inch between their shoulders in the front seat. Before the word *divorce* splintered into its seven selves, each one an armadillo that may or may not have existed.

Hala Alyan is a Palestinian American writer and clinical psychologist whose work has appeared in the *New York Times*, *Guernica*, and elsewhere. Her poetry collections have won the Arab American Book Award and the Crab Orchard Series. Her debut novel *Salt Houses* (Houghton Mifflin Harcourt, 2017) was longlisted for the Aspen Words Literary Prize.

Karen Donovan : A Gothic Tale

[From *Moon City Review*, 2017]

The knob at the back of his neck didn't hurt at all, so he didn't mention it to anyone at first. Excepting a slight wince when what was developing there broke the skin, he was pain free, but we were close to panic. We drew near, but his body was so hot we had to take turns holding him. It seemed that the growth exuded a natural opiate, because even when he lost all movement in his limbs, even when the prognosis was clear, he remained upbeat. Toward the end we had trouble understanding his speech, an unearthly mixture of humming and growling. *Shhhh, I'm growing my wings*, he might have been saying. But that is not what happened.

Karen Donovan discovered a vintage *Webster's* dictionary owned by her grandfather, fell in love with the illustrations, and wrote *Aard-vark to Axolotl* (Etruscan Press, 2018), in which this fiction appears. Her two books of poetry are *Your Enzymes Are Calling the Ancients* (Persea Books, 2016), which won the Lexi Rudnitsky / Editor's Choice Award, and *Fugitive Red* (University of Massachusetts Press, 1999), which won the Juniper Prize. From 1985 to 2005 she co-edited *A Magazine of Paragraphs*, a journal of very short prose published by Oat City Press. She lives in East Providence, Rhode Island.

Maxim Loskutoff :
Get Down, Stay Down

[From *Sou'wester*, Spring 2017]

Coach keeps his state championship trophy on the very front edge of his desk where it nearly topples over into your lap when he gets agitated, due to his fat gut jammed against the other side. His office isn't much more than a closet, but he could move the desk out a couple feet from the wall. I think he likes it. I think he likes getting squeezed into tight places because it reminds him of his small, sweaty, lost triumphs. But I'm just the kid in the chair before morning practice, watching the trophy wobble and thinking about braining him with it and also the careful, submissive way I'll have to pick it up if it does fall.

When he pairs us off for grappling he gets right down next to my ear and looks across at Kevin Aguilar who I'm going against at 220 and says, *"Get down, stay down,"* as if he's the voice inside my head talking to Kevin. Then he hustles his fat ass around to the other side, red shorts swishing, and says the same thing in Kevin's ear so now it's me who's being told to get down and stay down. Which I do not like, and I come in so hard at Kevin's knees that I lift him up off the mat and know I'm going to have to apologize because it's practice even as I'm twisting and slamming his body down onto the stretched vinyl.

"This shouldn't even be legal," my sister said at state last year after Al Tranchina got concussed so bad they had to stretcher him out in a neck brace. She's right, but all through Trig I think with satisfaction about the dull, thwocking sound Kevin's skull made. And he's a friend. It's this pressed-in feeling that gets me. The desks aren't big enough. The air conditioning never works. And Mrs. Price's marker doing cosine on the whiteboard hits a frequency that I associate with needles down around my ball-sack. Next time she picks up the blue marker I'm going to scoot out of my desk, charge up the aisle, and pop-and-chop her against the corner of the trashcan.

Soh cah toa!

Coach says wrestling is like life in that it's you against everyone else. I followed him out to the parking lot one night after a meet and the back window of his Lincoln Continental was busted out and covered with an old, red, varsity blanket. His bellybutton protrudes like a giant nipple against his Spartans polo shirt. When he exhales, it's moldy, old man, Skoal breath; breath of despair. It might be what the heart of the world smells like after we're done with it. My sister is always talking about the trash island in the ocean. How it's bigger than the United States now. New York to California all on trash. The next great American road trip, she calls it, which I'm guessing is a pretty good joke. She's going to college next year. On her calendar she marks off the days with big black Xs.

Most of the reason I joined the wrestling team was so I'd have something to do when someone makes a crack about her weight. I have to listen to her cry in the bathroom in the morning. It's glandular. I swear to God it is. The only friend she has is her Spanish teacher, Señor Byrne. She spends all her free time in his classroom. He's a scrawny little rapid-blinker with a stuffed, red and yellow parrot hanging over his desk. He talks to me in Spanish even though he's about the whitest person I've ever seen. The teachers here are idiots, too. His door is usually open, but today, when I go to find her, it's closed. Standing in front of it I don't hear a sound exactly, but I'm suddenly gripped by an icy, sucking dread like something terrible and deformed is about to come staggering out so I don't even knock. I just push it open.

The lights are off and it's dim except for weak sunrays slotting in through the blinds. My sister is up on Señor Byrne's lap behind the desk, facing him, dwarfing him, her shirt pushed up, his glasses askew and way down the bridge of his nose so he's gaping over them at her wide, flushed chest. Her bra is still on but it's sort of pinched and crammed off to the side so her breasts are spilling out. Her nipples, which I guess are the only parts that matter, are lit by the sun. All I'd wanted was to ask her if she'd had lunch. We used to always get lunch together. The goddamn parrot overhead looks much too real in the dimness, like it's about to come to life, about to squawk, *"Pretty bird! Pretty bird!"*

Both of them jolt, and Señor Byrne gives me these big, desperate eyes as his hands try to cover up half the room. He wouldn't tip 150 soaking wet. I could pick him up and put his head through the floor. They'd need tools to get him out. They'd have to tear the whole building in half. Just say the word, Coach. My sister is jerking her chin at the door and hissing at me, or maybe she's saying something. I'm not sure if my ears are working right. She's got her nipples halfway back in. There's a lot of buzzing. My stomach is slipping down my leg. Look at those shrimpy hands. I know the moves. I'll put him down so hard he comes out the other side. China, like she and I used to pretend back when we were kids digging in the yard. Back when I didn't know what an ankle pick was and she'd never heard of the Great Pacific

Maxim Loskutoff

Garbage Patch. When it hadn't started to hurt to get up. When none of this would've been imaginable.

Maxim Loskutoff is the author of *Come West and See* (W.W. Norton, 2018). His stories have appeared in *Ploughshares*, *The Southern Review*, and *Fiction*. A graduate of NYU's MFA program, he was the recipient of a Global Writing Fellowship in Abu Dhabi and the M Literary Fellowship in Bangalore. Other honors include the Nelson Algren Award, a James Merrill Fellowship, and an arts grant from The Elizabeth George Foundation. He has worked as a carpenter, field organizer, and writing teacher, among many other things. He lives in western Montana.

Reginald Gibbons :
Dead Man's Things

[From *An Orchard in the Street* (BOA Editions, 2017)]

Well, change from a dead man's pockets, for instance—a quarter would be a powerful frightening object to have in your hand when we were kids if it came from the pocket of a dead man, like that guy shot by police whose change spilled onto the sidewalk when he fell, that time.

Somehow these coins were more powerful than the money of a man of no power who wasn't dead yet, but only dying, like that Nigerian student who came to Chicago and sold ice cream from a truck in the summer evenings and who was shot in the neighborhood and people called 911 and waited and waited till the police and an ambulance came after a while and he had bled out onto the sidewalk while some kids darted up now and then to take ice cream and money from his little truck.

You had a dead man's hat for a while, bought at a garage sale for two dollars, a beautiful gray Stetson with a rattle-snake-skin band. He hadn't been wearing it when he was killed in a car crash, and his brother didn't want to keep it. You have some things of a dead man who was your kin—

your uncle—and whom you loved because of what he was and what he had done even though you only saw him a few times in your life. An old small Persian rug, that he had bought in 1930-something from a stranger who'd come to his door and asked your uncle if he'd give him five dollars for it, which he did. That man too, dead now too, certainly.

You have only one thing from your uncle's father—your grandfather—which is the way you used to set the knights on the chessboard, facing not ahead toward the coming battle in which they are likely to perish but at their queen and king, like he taught you when you were little.

You've got some clothes of one dead man—a few things given to you by his son, pretty worn out now. You didn't know him well but you admired him. When you put that red wool shirt of his on, you sometimes think of him and thank him for helping you onward after he stopped coming with the rest of us. And other clothes—even a coat, the most sacred of all clothing, given to you by the widow of another man, a friend who was another uncle to you and whom you loved.

Of your other grandfather maybe you have the way you put out your hand when you say certain things, or maybe even the way you say them, who knows, you'll never know, he died when you were two.

And from the man whose coat you used to wear only once in a while in winter, and that later you gave to someone else who loved him, too, you have the greatest thing—the words you speak if you read aloud from his books. And the shape of your breath and the beating of your heart as you read, and the space you're inside when you're in his work and away from everything else, or maybe his books take you into everything else; and you marvel at what he had and wonder where did he get that? Did dead men or women give him that? Which ones? Or who did he take it from, darting up near him as that writer lay bleeding out in one way or another from his body or his body of work before the police came to arrest him for having bled or readers standing around him turned their backs and said nothing? Did he grab a coin he took from a dying writer's books and shove it in his pocket till it was his time to spend it?

Reginald Gibbons has published ten books of poems, including *Last Lake* (U of Chicago, 2016), and three of fiction, most recently *An Orchard in the Street* (BOA Editions Ltd, 2017). His *Creatures of a Day* was a Finalist for the National Book Award in poetry. He has also published a book on poetry, *How Poems Think* (U of Chicago, 2015) and translations of Sophocles (Oxford UP and Princeton UP), Luis Cernuda (Sheep Meadow) and other poets. He teaches at Northwestern University, where he is currently director of Northwestern's new MFA+MA in creative writing and English.

Lori Sambol Brody :
The Truth About Alaskan Rivers

[From *The Forge Literary Magazine*, March 6, 2017]

Afterwards, we try to do trig homework, but Taylor's still upset about what happened in gym class, so he turns on the TV. In the middle of the doom-and-gloom local news, the newscasters start talking about the Freeway Sniper.

I can't believe anyone would do that, I say.

And he says in his sweet I'm-not-from-Cali accent, He does it because it's easy.

I pretend the steady shhh of the 10 Freeway outside the window is the sound of a river running in the backyard and we aren't in this tacky apartment he shares with his mother, the floors trembling when someone walks on the catwalks and cigarette smoke leaking from cracks around the medicine cabinet. An apartment building like the one I live in, only we have a pool blooming algae-green in the courtyard.

What do you mean? I finally say.

And he says, Let me show you.

He goes into his mother's room and comes out carrying this long ass gun like it's a baby in his arms and I look at him like what the hell.

Relax, he says. It's just a rifle.

Well, yeah, I know it's a fuckin' rifle.

It doesn't have bullets in it.

Why do you even have a rifle?

Used to go shooting with my dad back in Texas. Come on.

I stand up, pull my crop top down, attempting to cover my stomach. I should go, I say, mom will kill me if I'm late for dinner.

Come on, he repeats.

His eyes are what made me chase him. They're turquoise, like those Alaskan rivers I've seen in travel magazines, the rivers running from glaciers to ocean. Eyes I thought I could ride like a raft until the rapids whirled me away. But now his eyes shoot past me and for a moment it's like he's checked out of his body. Like during the basketball game today when Jimmy Creek and his crew surrounded him and he went to that place and was icy cold.

And if I'm honest I'm a little scared of him when he's like that, although he tells me, Honey, I'd never hurt you.

I say now, Ok, but be quick.

He leads me out of the apartment up to the roof. There, someone's dragged up a pair of mismatched lounge chairs and faced them west, although a scrim of apartment buildings blocks any view of the Pacific. A red Solo cup stands on one chair, filled with soggy cigarette butts. The gravel roof crunches below my boots.

Taylor's already at the edge. There's no wall or fence, just the edge dropping off. He lies on his stomach. The rifle by his side. Lie down, he says. I pause. His hand grabs my wrist and pulls me down.

The raw edges of the gravel dig into my bare stomach.

Palms line the frontage street Taylor lives on, the trees untrimmed and wearing shrouds of dead leaves around their trunks. I can see the freeway between the palms. All eight lanes, the closest thing that L.A. has to a real river. Cars rushing, each blurring into the next. Everything in motion.

Beyond the 10, beyond rooftops, mountains rise purple and brown. There, I imagine, narrow roads twist through oaks and picture windows reflect the sun like diamonds.

The gun lies between us.

Why did you bring the gun? I say and I don't know if the tightness in my chest is from lying on sharp gravel or the rising exhaust or something else.

Just to show you.

He takes the gun and aims it at the freeway, his finger on the trigger, one hand curling around the barrel to support it. I take a sharp breath. Those same hands peeled off my jeans, pinned mine over my head as he moved inside me, not 30 minutes ago.

No wonder the sniper thinks he's so powerful, he says.

There's no bullets, right?

The safety's on.

Let's go back, I say.

Not yet. You try. He hands me the rifle. It's heavier than I thought. He shows me how to hold it, close one eye to look through the sight. Be careful, if you shoot it's going to kick back.

My hands shake.

It's hard to see the people in the cars. Shadows through the windows, like images in dreams that you can't hold onto after you wake.

Look at them, he says. Nobodies. His breath is hot against my neck; I imagine him breathing a hole in my skin as if he's melting ice.

Everything's blurry and I realize I'm crying.

Just aim through a window, he says.

His blue eyes gleam cold, and I remember that those Alaskan rivers run so turquoise because they've got all that crap in them that's left when a glacier melts. Glacial soup, they call it. Dirt and rocks.

All you need to do is pull the trigger, he says.

My finger cramps. This freeway crosses the country. Millions of people flying up and down its lanes, to the Pacific, to the Atlantic. Everyone going somewhere. And me so still.

Lori Sambol Brody grew up in tacky Los Angeles apartments and now lives in the Santa Monica Mountains with her family. She dislikes the word "Cali." Her short fiction has appeared in *SmokeLong Quarterly*, *Tin House Flash Fridays*, *New Orleans Review*, *The Rumpus*, *Little Fiction*, *Necessary Fiction*, *Sundog Lit*, and elsewhere. She is working on a short story collection.

Lydia Davis :
The Visitor

[From *The Masters Review*, Featured Fiction (online), June 2, 2017]

Sometime in the early summer, a stranger will come and take up residence in our house. Although we have not met him, we know he will be bald, incontinent, speechless, and nearly completely unable to help himself. We don't know exactly how long he will stay, relying entirely on us for food, clothing, and shelter.

Our situation reminds me that a leathery-skinned old Indian gentleman once spent several months with my sister in London. At first he slept in a tent in her back yard. Then he moved into the house. Here he made it his project to rearrange the many books in the house, which were in no particular order. He decided upon categories—mystery, history, fiction—and surrounded himself with clouds of smoke from his cigarettes as he worked. He explained his system in correct but halting English to anyone who came into the room. Several years later he died suddenly and painfully in a London hospital. For religious reasons, he had refused all treatment.

This Indian visitor of my sister's also reminds me of another old man—the very old father of a friend of mine.

He had once been a professor of economics. He was old and deaf even when my friend was a child. Later he could not contain his urine, laughed wildly and soundlessly during his daughter's wedding, and when asked to say a few words rose trembling and spoke about Communism. This man is now in a nursing home. My friend says he is smaller every year.

Like my friend's father, our visitor will have to be bathed by us, and will not use the toilet. We have appointed a small, sunny room for him next to ours, where we will be able to hear him if he needs help during the night. Some day, he may repay us for all the trouble we will go to, but we don't really expect it. Although we have not yet met him, he is one of the few people in the world for whom we would willingly sacrifice almost anything.

Lydia Davis is a short story writer, novelist, and translator. She has published six short story collections, most recently *Can't and Won't* (2014), and one novel, *The End of the Story* (1995), along with a collected volume, *The Collected Stories of Lydia Davis*, which includes her 2007 National Book Award-nominated *Varieties of Disturbances*. She has also published numerous translations of French literature and philosophy into English, including works by Marcel Proust, Maurice Blanchot, and Gustave Flaubert. Davis has won a Guggenheim Fellowship, a MacArthur Fellowship, and the 2013 Man Booker International Prize. She received her BA from Barnard College, and is a professor of English and writer-in-residence at SUNY Albany.

Kaj Tanaka :
In Dugave

[From *New South Journal*, Micro Prose, February 2017]

Tonight, as we walked back to our hostel in the little outskirt where we are staying, we saw a dog on the road, and beneath that dog we saw a second dog and beneath that second dog we saw the deep and unending darkness. We felt uneasy about this entire package, so we crossed to the other side of the street—passing now—we on the left, the dog on the right. It was only we and the dog and the streetlights, and beneath the sidewalk there was a second sidewalk with more bright neon streetlights beneath another dark sky and beneath all of that, the dragon, sleeping beneath this city, drinking milk from the old women who remember to throw gallons of it into wells or flush it down their toilets. And after the dog passed us, the silence and the stars and the two of us lost in the strange houses of this neighborhood, and beneath those houses two more and two more people and so on. And finally, coming back to our tiny room, our faces nearly touching in the glow of our little bedroom lamp and, later, two more faces hovering around us, none of them our own.

Kaj Tanaka teaches creative writing at the Harris County Jail in Houston, Texas. His stories have been nominated for the Pushcart Prize, featured in *Longform*, and selected for *Wigleaf*'s Top 50 (Very) Short Fictions. He is the nonfiction editor for *BULL Magazine*. You can tweet to him @kajtanaka. kajtanaka.com

Kaj Tanaka :
The Night Is Where It Throws You

[From *(b)OINK*, issue 3, March 2017]

He looks up at me over his beer and asks if I know where he can get a woman—for money, he clarifies. He seems embarrassed to ask. He says this is always the awkward part—finding a woman. I tell him I'm not sure where he can get a woman for money in this town. I tell him he can pay me if he wants, and I'll be his woman. I'm not what he usually goes for. I ask him what he goes for. *Just someone to talk to*, he says, *a woman, though.* His lips are thin and unnatural looking. His father burned them off with an iron, he tells me. He asks if I mind his burned lips. *Just someone where I don't need to worry that they're mine. I don't like feeling jealous, and I don't like to be alone at the end of the night.* And so I tell him to stay with me at my place. I take his hand. I tell him he doesn't have a choice now. I tell him I won't run off if he pays me; he smiles and shakes my hand.

He drinks fast. I try to keep up, but I am getting too drunk, so I lay off. The more he drinks, the more money he gives me—mostly small bills. I take them. I put them in my pocket. He keeps telling me to buy something nice. He says that I am the nicest thing he has bought in a long time. I tell him that I am a person and he can't buy me. But he keeps saying he bought me fair and square—the same way he buys a plane ticket online, the same way he buys his cowboy boots.

Some of my friends from school see me sitting next to him and they come over. They try to get me out of there because they want to protect me. I tell them to go, but they linger in the corner of the bar like a smell; and when we leave, they begin to trail us. They keep their distance and maybe they think I can't see them, but I can. I see them skulking in my periphery, haunting me like snakes.

He talks about money mostly. He has a lot of money, he says. *A single man doesn't need much.* He eats, he drinks, he fucks—lots of guys go broke doing those things, but he has cheap taste. I don't say anything. He's told me several times how he isn't paying me to talk.

At every bar he sees the ghosts of past lives—women who look like other women, drinks that remind him of other drinks, bartenders whose names he swears he knows but doesn't. He seems to know this town. I ask him if he comes here often, and he tells me to shut my mouth. He orders me special drinks—drinks he can connect to his personal history. I drink them all.

He takes me to the ATM and asks me how much I want. A thousand, I say. He tries to withdraw five thousand, but the ATM limit is $400. I tell him I'll settle for that. He tells me I'm a good one. He tells me I'm worth five thousand dollars, and he'll pay me the rest later. I see my friends fading through the night, then, drifting past the windows outside the bodega. I see them in the shadows. I see them behind every streetlight. He takes my chin in his hands and kisses me with his scarred lips and they feel like the skin of a finger, like a clenched fist. We get into his car because he wants to see some water. He says he knows a place. He hands me an unopened 750 of whiskey in a plastic bottle. He tells me to drink. I crack it open. It's bad stuff. He drinks some. And the road is the spine of a black bull and the night is where it throws you.

Down by the river, the water sounds like wind. He tells me there is a waterfall nearby, and that's the sound I'm hearing. He says he used to come here as a boy. I think of water hammering rock. I think of water beating down on my head until I have holes, perfect round holes like on those rocks. The water is so loud that I don't hear anything. It doesn't take long. He's usually more of a giver, he says, but tonight he's tired. I tell him I don't mind. He keeps talking about my body, about how pretty I am and how smart. My friends never tell me things like that. And when I sit up, my friends are there. I can see them in the darkness—smiling behind the rocks, laughing at me. Their hearts cowardly, their love like mayflies, born in the water.

Kaj Tanaka teaches creative writing at the Harris County Jail in Houston, Texas. His stories have been nominated for the Pushcart Prize, featured in *Longform*, and selected for *Wigleaf*'s Top 50 (Very) Short Fictions. He is the nonfiction editor for *BULL Magazine*. You can tweet to him @kajtanaka. kajtanaka.com

Desiree Cooper :
The Good Hours

[From *Electric Literature, Okey-Panky*, August 2017]

I had for my winter evening walk—
No one at all with whom to talk
— Robert Frost

It's nine p.m. and the night stretches before me like a glacier. Despite the fact that it's started to snow again, I pull on my fleece for an evening walk. These days, I walk until the cold slows my heart and I can sleep without nightmares. Sometimes I have to walk two or three times before dawn to stay in front of the dread.

There is a plague upon our house. It's making the thin wallpaper curl, the tongue-and-groove floors moan. We have lost our grasp on tomorrow. We pretend to still have jobs as we come and go, waving at the neighbors. But we all know that this infection will spread. At least once a week during my walks, I see a new sign: "Bank Owned," or "Auction." Overnight, a white document appears on a neighbor's front door. The opposite of lamb's blood—a sign that God will not protect them.

I've learned to detect the early signs. The yard service is the first to go. Grass invades the cracks in the driveway. Leaves mound like fresh graves. After a night of snow, sidewalks go unshoveled. Windows shutter. Porch lights shine all day long.

Tonight, I say vespers for the Babcocks and Lindsays. In six months, a year, there will be no survivors left on our block. I wonder if this is how it feels during epidemics. Each house under quarantine, neighbors peering from behind curtains, hiding signs of financial ruin. People vanishing without a good-bye.

In October, Theresa Madding had an estate sale. I went for the same reason we go to wakes: to check out the condition of the body. The Madding house was in surprisingly good repair. Their downfall must have been swift; there would be no trouble finding a buyer for a short sale. As I scoured Theresa's possessions, I was grateful that most of the people streaming in on that dreary autumn morning were not from the neighborhood. It's against the unspoken code for us to circle the pyre of our neighbors' belongings.

On Theresa's dining room table among three different sets of dishes (how much china does one family really need?) sat the most exquisite tureen. Williamsburg blue, delicate white flowers laced with gold. Even then, I knew we probably were going to lose our home and the tureen would not survive our journey into the unknown. But in the moment, it felt like an inoculation of hope—a talisman to keep the infection from spreading to us.

I snatched it up quickly and darted to the checkout. And that's when I ran into Theresa. It's a horrible slap, to be caught paying pennies for your neighbors' belongings.

"Hello," I mumbled, angry at her for attending her own funeral.

"My tureen!" she gushed. "We used that so many times during the holidays. You're going to love it." She emitted the strange glee of someone who has lost everything.

"Thank you," I said. I should have said more.

Once I got the tureen in the car, I started crying and couldn't stop. We never used it. When our real estate agent came to size up our house, she noticed the tureen in the china cabinet. I made her take it home.

Tonight, the air stings. The snow creaks beneath my feet, profane. No dogs bark curiously. Hardly any doors bear holiday wreaths. This year, there have been no parties to spill their light onto the stark drifts. Where is the sound of the children next door practicing carols on their violins?

The cold gnaws at my toes. My lips feel useless. I want to cry but the frigid air has dried my eyes. This is somehow my fault. I should have saved more money. I should have left town a long time ago. I should have majored in something else. I should have married better, or had one fewer child.

Beneath a dim streetlight, I turn and repent. All the windows are blackened this winter's eve. The good hours have gone.

Desiree Cooper is a 2015 Kresge Artist Fellow, former attorney, and Pulitzer Prize-nominated journalist. Her debut collection of flash fiction, *Know the Mother* (Wayne State University Press, 2016), has won numerous awards for short story and cover design, including a 2017 Next Generation Indie Book Award. Cooper's fiction, poetry, and essays have appeared in *Callaloo*, *Hypertext Review*, *Best African American Fiction 2010*, and *This is the Place*, among other online and print publications. Cooper was a founding board member of Cave Canem, a national residency for emerging black poets. She is currently a Kimbilio Fellow, a national residency for African American fiction writers.

Kate Keleher :
Sweater

[From *Crazyhorse*, No. 91, Spring 2017]

The moms and dads of Eden Prairie gathered at the Kinney's house, dressed as cats and superheroes for the most part. Ned was Pig Latin. He wore a pig mask and wrote Carpe Diem on his stomach, which he flashed at everyone throughout the night. His wife Susan was a Ceiling Fan, which is to say she wore a shirt that said "Go Ceilings." She was not very beautiful, but she was smart and funny, and I liked Ned all the more for being with someone like her. The babysitter got sick. Susan left early. Then Ned was crawling on all fours, oinking and nuzzling my legs under the table where I sat.

"E pluribus oink'em," he said, head between my knees.

I lifted the tablecloth and hissed, "Ut-way ed-nay."

My friend Cheri, the other single mom in town, sat beside me chewing gum and talking to her stoner son on the phone.

"Who are you with, honey?" Where are you going? Promise me you won't drive." By the time Ned retreated under the table she had missed him completely.

If I was still married, I imagine I would be friends with Ned and Susan. They have signs for Democratic candidates on their lawn and a wind chime made out of spoons.

Ned was in the kitchen, looking for ice. My eyes were warm and blurry from the beer.

"How are you?" I asked.

"Holly!" he said. "Quick, how would you describe the breasts of a robot?"

"Metallic?"

"Robust." He laughed at his own joke with splayed teeth and boozy breath.

The other parents were dancing and sloshing against the walls and countertops like teenagers. Someone turned off the lights in the living room. Ned danced with me and cupped my hips with cold hands.

When we walked through the town center, a car drove by with people gesturing and yelling to us either *Liar!* or *Hi there!*

"Just some people from the PTA," he said.

Then I walked him home. He toed an upturned tricycle on the front lawn.

"We have six now," he said. "Four boys, two girls. What we lack in quality we make up for in quantity."

On the porch, a thin pink sweater lay crumpled on the bench. We sat in separate rocking chairs, creaking in opposition. My eyes still felt hot and I closed them, focused on the new November chill like a cool cloth on my neck. When I opened my eyes he was looking at me.

I went home and paid the sitter. In bed, suspended between sleep and wakefulness, I thought of the light pink sweater. What would it look like? How would it feel? How would it hang around my neck?

Kate Keleher's story "Sweater" won the 2017 *Crazyhorse* Short-Short Fiction contest. In 2017, she danced in Art Haus' Rite of Spring Ballet and worked on productions with Trademark, Shelley Lewis Films, and the San Francisco Dance Film Festival. Her short play *Sign Language*, staged by PlayGround SF at Berkeley Repertory Theatre, won the March 2018 People's Choice Award. She is based in Oakland, California.

Chance Dibben :
Magic Arrow

[From *matchbook* June 2017]

The time traveler will always land in the volcano. Her death will be as instant as her transmission to the past. The scientists will remain gravely unaware of their miscalculations. As a kid, she dreamed of space. Pinned bugs to boards. Took apart computers. This was her escape. This was her talent. She was born into a rough family outside Akron. Her father died when she was nine in a hunting accident, her mother a manic-depressive. She had to grow up fast and perhaps grew up too fast. This might explain the drugs and crime, but it would be irresponsible to draw her arc in bold, clean lines.

When they offered her a deal, she took it without hesitation or consideration of the consequences. This was her chance to be a part of history, to pin a bug to a board, to be the bug looked at for the rest of, ahem, time.

The scientists will always run her through a bevy of tests and feats of strength. Her curiosity and aptitude will always separate her from the other candidates. She will always become family with them, falling in love with a lanky gray-haired particle physicist. They will always slowly fall in love and keep it hidden because it breaks protocol. He will always give her his father's war watch. She will always enter the portal with a secret smile, her fingers crossed. She will always land in the volcano.

Perhaps you think she can be saved. Perhaps you can fix the scientists' equations or steer her away from a short period of crime. You want to break her father's car so he can't go on the hunting trip or have him bend down to scratch his leg just before the bullet is fired. You want the mother to keep her job or find a better one with health insurance. I'm sorry. The father will always be shot by his friend, a heavy mosquito tickling his trigger finger. The mother will always feel a growing storm in her head. The time traveler will always land in the volcano. She will always poke the dead caterpillar writhing with ants. She will always swallow too much pool water and get a nosebleed. She will always have ice cream in the car with her mother and father, swarmed with feelings of security. She will always be cradled as a baby, leaving the hospital, her whole life ahead of her.

Chance Dibben is a writer, photographer, and performer living in Lawrence, Kansas. His poems and shorts have appeared in *Split Lip Magazine*, *Reality Beach*, *Horsethief*, *Yes Poetry*, *Atlas and Alice*, *matchbook*, *Hobart*, as well as others. Find him at chancedibben on Twitter. chancedibben.com

Matt Bell :
The Architect's Gambit

[From *Booth X*, 2017]

Years before the abandonment was announced, the older had already been building the dollhouse for the younger, and so the younger said she would not give herself up to be left until she was allowed to play with it just once. When at last it was complete, the parents granted the younger a mere hour to play, after which they promised the sisters would both be taken away. But in the odd ticking of that hour the younger found a new world, one of fast incident tucked inside slow time, and inside the dollhouse each room was complete with tiny furniture, each closet stocked with tiny clothes that fit the paper dolls she found sleeping in the beds, one doll for the older and one for the younger.

There were no dolls of her parents and the younger found she did not care. It was not her parents she loved. It was not her parents she had dreamed of moving through the rooms of the dollhouse.

In fact, she was glad her parents were gone, she realized, as she pressed a knuckle of coal into the miniature working stove, as she shuttered the windows against the coming storm the older let fall from a water can held above the house. What delight, to be in such a well-built house, even if only in play! There was a tiny mirror in the bedroom that was like the younger's bedroom—the one she shared with the older child—and when the younger put her eye to the window she could see her eye reflected in the mirror hung on that room's wall, her eye reflected as big as a god's, seeming to stare down at the dolls while they slept in their tiny nightshirts.

The younger watched a long time. She had known hunger and cold but now she thought she knew happiness too. She thought she could give her happiness to the doll younger, to the doll older, by watching them and loving them. She had been promised only an hour but now she thought that hour skipped, stuttered, grew long. It was not real time but story time, imagined time, and when at last the tap on her shoulder came, the younger sighed, because now she knew it was another time, time for her and the older to be taken to the woods, where they would be left.

One more look, she told herself. A look that lasts so long.

The younger doll was still sleeping, as was the older. This was in her imagination—they were only paper, after all—but it did not feel so. The younger thought she could see the movement of their dreams. The younger thought they could be made to sleep forever.

This was a good house, she thought, because it was made only for children. A younger and an older.

But when she thought the word *younger*, she had stopped knowing if it meant her or her doll.

The tap on her shoulder returned, and so the younger took her eye away from the window—slowly, so that she could watch the god-eye escape the bedroom mirror—and when she stood and turned she found that she had to blink her eyes rapidly so they might readjust to the sunny play-room. The person who had tapped her was not her father or mother but a stranger to her, and for a moment the younger was afraid—afraid even though she knew what her mother and father had planned—until she understood that this person was her older, grown. The younger looked down at herself and saw that she was still a child, the same child she'd always been, beautiful and lovely and in dire need of saving. The new older smiled and took her small hand. This is one of the ways a child can be kept safe, the older said. And then in the other room the older showed the younger the bones of their parents, almost dust, still waiting in their bed for the younger to willingly agree to be abandoned by these people, the man and woman who had made her, who had once been meant to love her most, in a bigger and emptier house of their own.

Matt Bell is the author of the novels *Scrapper* and *In the House Upon the Dirt Between the Lake and the Woods*, as well as the short story collection *A Tree or a Person or a Wall* (Soho Press, 2016), a non-fiction book about the classic video game *Baldur's Gate II*, and several other titles. His writing has appeared in the *New York Times*, *Tin House*, *Conjunctions*, *Fairy Tale Review*, *American Short Fiction*, and many other publications. A native of Michigan, he teaches in the Creative Writing Program at Arizona State University.

Mary-Jane Holmes :
Postpartum

[From *Reflex Fiction*, Autumn 2017]

She'd mottled like a gull's egg in the carrying of her, left the bairn newly birthed, howling in twitch grass by the river; returned to her wheel to draft wool skeins, skirts crusted brown, foot against the treadle, fast and even.

Her husband found it, batted the flies from the cord freshly cut, took the bawling bantling in his great flat palms and the baby calmed, took to suckling his knuckle still sweet with wood sap.

He pressed his wife to take the infant back, held her raw hands, once as smooth as corn-silk; called her *harvest moon* as he'd done summers ago in the stubble of the twelve-acre. But with each appeal, she plucked a sheaf of her hair and taking up her spindle, twisted the shafts to a silver ply that coiled like steel around her.

The child whined, beat the lattice of his ribs for love or hunger so he fossicked a horse bridle to hold her and that was how he worked—daughter hoyed across his back in quarry and field until spring, when driving his pony string from shoreline to pithead he unhitched the girl, for the bridle was needed for the journey; left her at her mother's feet playing with the rovings that fell from her spinner, hoping her laughter might feather his wife's heart.

When he returned, a hundred gold sovereigns lighting his wallet, a wattled crib swinging from his side, he found the farm deserted but tied from the spinning wheel, a noil of thread which he followed past alder groves and drying sheds to the banks of the river. There was his daughter at the water's edge: naked, cough-kinked. He scooped her up, swaddled her as best he could but nothing, not even his knuckle dipped in bee-bread stemmed the crying.

Then he saw it: a shimmer of cloth caught in shingle on the bank. He unhooked it. So soft. Delicate as shell. Held to his cheek he heard it sigh something akin to the crepitation of hay, felt its weft of eye and limb upon him as he wrapped the child within it and lay her cooing in the crib.

Mary-Jane Holmes has been published in such places as *Myslexia*, *The Journal of Compressed Creative Arts*, *Prole*, *The Tishman Review*, *The Lonely Crowd*, and *The Best Small Fictions 2016*. She is the winner of the 2017 Bridport Poetry Prize, the Martin Starkie Poetry Prize, the Bedford International Poetry Prize, and the Dromineer Fiction Prize. Her debut poetry collection *Siren Call* was published by Glasgow-based Pindrop Press in 2018. Mary-Jane is chief editor of Fish Publishing Ireland, editorial consultant at *The Well Review*, and director of the Creative Writing Programme, Casa Ana, Spain. She holds a Master of Studies (distinction) in creative writing from Kellogg College, Oxford. mary-janeholmes.com

Gwen E. Kirby :

Shit Cassandra Saw That She Didn't Tell the Trojans Because at that Point Fuck Them Anyway

[From *SmokeLong Quarterly*, Issue Fifty-Five, January 2, 2017]

Lightbulbs.

Penguins.

Velcro.

Claymation. The moon made out of cheese.

Tap dancing.

Yoga.

Twizzlers. Mountain Dew. Jello. Colors she can eat with her eyes.

Methamphetamine.

Bud Lite.

T-shirts. Thin and soft, they pass from person to person, men to women, each owner slipping into a team—Yankees,

Warriors—and out again with no bloodshed, no thought to allegiance or tribe. And the words! Profusions of nonsense. The Weather Is Here, Wish You Were Fine. Chemists Do It on the Table Periodically. Cut Class Not Frogs. Words everywhere and for everyone, for nothing but a joke, for the pleasure of them, a world so careless with its words. And not just on t-shirts. Posters. Water bottles. Newspapers. Junk mail. Bumper stickers. Lists. Top ten Halloween costumes for your dog as modeled by this corgi. Top ten times a monkey's facial expression perfectly summed up your thoughts on NAFTA. Top ten things your boyfriend *wishes* you would do in bed but is too afraid to say. Cassandra has not noticed a lack of men telling women what to do. Perhaps this will be a pleasure of the future, a male desire that goes *un*spoken. A desire that is only a desire, and not a command.

Then there are the small words, the private words, hidden within romance novels, mysteries, thrillers, science fiction, fantasy. Heaving bosoms, astronauts, and ape men. Pulp paperbacks that live brief but fiery lives, the next torrent of words so swift behind they must sell or be destroyed, only enough space on the shelf for the new.

Broadway.

Chekov.

Klonopin.

Dentistry.

Density.

And lives, of course. Cassandra would rather see only the fictions, the objects, the colored plastic oddities of the future, but she must see lives as well. Here are two little girls. They sit in the dirt and dig at a boulder. When it is finally unearthed, the possibilities! A passage to the underworld, a buried treasure, a colony of fairies—anything but dirt. It is essential that they will never succeed, never dig up the boulder, and of course they don't. Their plastic shovels move the dirt aside; new dirt, dusty and thin, blows across their eyes, fills the small spaces they've made. One of the girls becomes an engineer. One is raped by her college boyfriend. Some visions show nothing new at all. This second girl will run a bakery on an island where she loves to hike. She will have three children, all boys, and she will die when she is quite old and quite unwilling to go. Her boys will have lives too. Everyone does. Lives on fast-forward, silent, even the best life, even her own, swiftly boring.

Cassandra is tired of running at wooden horses with nothing but the flame of the smallest match.

She is tired of speaking to listening ears. The listening ears of the men who think her mad drive her to madness. She wishes they would let her keep her silence or scream her knowledge alone, wishes she could move to an island and own a bird. She will never do this because she knows she never does.

It is said that Apollo gave Cassandra the gift of prophecy—this is true. It is said that, when she refused his advances, he spit in her mouth so that she would never again be believed. A virgin the same as a seduced woman the same as a violated woman the same as a willing woman, all women opening their mouths to watch snakes slither out and away.

Cassandra is *done*, full the fuck up, soul weary.

Still, as Troy is sacked, as she clings to the statue of Athena in the sacred temple, the marble of the legs cold no matter how tight she holds them, she cannot accept what she knows to be true. That soon, Ajax will arrive and rape her. He will smash the statue of the goddess she worships and curse his own life and worse, her goddess will not help her, will turn her shattered face away. Soon, Cassandra will be carried across the sea, made another man's concubine, bear twin boys, and be killed by Clytemnestra. But before this comes to pass, there are visions Cassandra burns to share with the women of Troy.

The women of Troy might listen. They know that Cassandra's curse is their curse as well. That Apollo spit in her mouth, but it was only spit.

Here is what she might show them.

Tampons.

Jeans.

Washing machines.

The cordless Hitachi Magic Wand.

Elastic hair ties.

Mace.

Epidurals.

A woman alone in a room, the door locked and no one expected.

And here is the best thing of all, the thing that makes Cassandra smile as the men storm her temple, exactly as she has always known they would. Someday, Trojan will not be synonymous with bravery or failure, betrayal or endurance, the most beautiful woman or the most foolish men. A Trojan will be carried in every hopeful wallet, pulled out with abashed confidence, slipped over the shaft, rolled to the base as awkwardly as a high school teacher with a banana. Perhaps the Trojan men would laugh if they knew, or be humiliated, or pause to think about the indifference of history and the hubris of the man who hopes to be remembered. But the women, once they saw that blue streamer unfurl, the women would rejoice, would wave it over their heads like a new flag, like a promise of better things to come.

Gwen E. Kirby's stories appear in *One Story*, *Guernica*, *Mississippi Review*, *Ninth Letter*, *New Ohio Review*, *SmokeLong Quarterly*, *New Delta Review*, and elsewhere. She won the 2017 DISQUIET Literary Prize for Fiction and has been awarded scholarships to the Rivendell Writers' Colony and the Sundress Academy for the Arts. A proud

Gwen E. Kirby

graduate of Carleton College, she received her MFA from Johns Hopkins University, and is finishing a doctorate at the University of Cincinnati. During the summers, she works for the Sewanee Young Writers' and Sewanee Writers' Conferences.

Best Small Fictions Finalists

Ghayath Almadhoun : How I became... (*The Guardian*)

Jules Archer : We Will Set Anything on Fire (*Maudlin House*)

Georgia Bellas : The Wolf Wears Jeggings (*MoonPark Review*)

Lori Sambol Brody : I Want to Believe the Truth Is Out There (*Jellyfish Review*)

Rowan Hisayo Buchanan : Juniper (*Fairy Tale Review*)

Kim Chinquee : Paper Dolls (from *Veer*, Ravenna Press)

Kim Chinquee : Halfway (from *Veer*, Ravenna Press)

Nicholas Cook : The Eclipse (*Lost Balloon*)

Nicholas Cook : The Family Myths (*Unbroken Journal*)

Emily Devane : The Hand That Wields The Priest (*Bath Flash Fiction Award*)

Todd Dillard : Myth in Which My Father Does Not Recreate the Moon Landing (*Atticus Review*)

Jacqueline Doyle : The Missing Girl (from *The Missing Girl*, Black Lawrence Press)

Jacqueline Doyle : Zig Zag (*Midway Journal*)

Austin Eichelberger : Places I Imagine My Wife (*Flash: The International Short-Short Story Magazine*)

Sarah Rose Etter : Sea Day (*Juked*)

Kathy Fish : The Once Mighty Fergusons (*New World Writing*)

Scott Garson : The Horoscope Writer (*Gulf Coast Online*)

Beth Gilstrap and Jim Warner : Discord No. 60 (*Third Point Press*)

Howie Good : Snap Krackle Pop (*Blink-Ink*)

Ihab Hassan : The Diner (from *Funny Bone: Flashing for Comic Relief*, Flash: The International Short-Short Story Press)

Brandon Hobson : Chicken (*NOON Annual*)

Jennifer A. Howard : Always Only Approximate (from *You on Mars: Failed Sci-Fi Stories*, The Cupboard Pamphlet LLP)

Ingrid Jendrzejewski : The Middle Ground (*Passages North*)

Jac Jenkins : Stigmeology (*Micro Madness*)

Timston Johnston : Pour Down Stinking (*WhiskeyPaper*)

Kate Jones : Jellyfish (*Reflex Fiction*)

Tara Laskowski : Hostage (*Alfred Hitchcock's Mystery Magazine*)

Elise Levine : Alice in the Field (*The Collagist*)

Jolene McIlwain : Drumming (*The Cincinnati Review*)

Frankie McMillan : The Geography of a Father (*The New Zealand Listener*)

Cole Meyer : Vesuvius (*SAND Journal*)

SPOTLIGHT on
Jellyfish Review

Best Small Fictions : On your website, you confess to having a soft spot for "beautiful things with stings"—a perfect description for powerful flash fiction! Tell us about the origins and ambitions of *Jellyfish Review*.

Christopher James, editor : *Jellyfish Review* began in 2015, when many magazines were introducing fees to submit. We understand why magazines need do this, but it's important too to have venues that don't charge, that are open to all writers, emerging, established, experimental, and everything else. There's a line (and I can't remember who said it) that the government doesn't need to censor books—the price of books censors books. We were worried something similar might happen to flash fiction. And so one night we set up the magazine. Thankfully, these days exciting new magazines are popping up all the time.

Our ambitions are to keep being a positive venue for flash fiction, to see the form grow, to build our community, and to watch our writers become stars.

BSF : *Jellyfish Review* made an impressive showing in this year's *Best Small Fictions* with two winning stories, Kathy Fish's "Collective Nouns for Humans in the Wild" and Melissa Goode's "It Falls," as well as a finalist and semi-finalist. How do these honored stories reflect your vision of the best contemporary flash and/or hybrid fiction?

CJ : Oh, we are in love with these two stories, and with these two writers as well. We got to know Melissa Goode a while ago, and she writes so crisply. "It Falls" begins with a couple holidaying in Berlin, overwhelmed by their visit to the Holocaust memorial. The man says they shouldn't have started with the memorial, they should've eased themselves in. She asks how you ease yourself into an apocalypse, and he says they should've gone to the pub first. It's astounding, and funny, and beautifully done.

Kathy Fish has been our hero for a long time, so we asked her to write something for our second anniversary. Then that awful shooting in Las Vegas happened. Kathy asked if we'd use "Collective Nouns for Humans in the Wild," which she'd written in direct response to that horrible day. Collective Nouns could be a story, a poem, or an essay, but more than any of these things it is a rallying call. I think a million people have probably already seen this. It's genuinely inspiring. We're biased, of course, but I challenge any writer to read this and not want to create their own beautiful impassioned cry from the heart.

BSF : As a writer, reader, and editor of flash fiction, what do you believe this form offers that no other genre quite satisfies?

CJ : A lifetime can change a person, so slowly we barely notice it happening. But a single instant can change a person, too. Like Joan Didion says, you sit down to dinner and life as you know it ends. Those are the instants we want to tell people about, to share, so other people can be changed the same way we were. Flash fiction—the best flash fiction— does this. It either captures one of those instants or becomes one of those instants. It changes people. Sometimes a little, sometimes a whole heap of lots! We've loved reading all the stories in *The Best Small Fictions 2018.* They've changed us, and we emerged from the other side of this anthology different, wiser, happier, and better.

SPOTLIGHT on Diane Williams

Best Small Fictions : Something that is noticeable about your work is the way it seems to seek the intimate spaces between words and action and feeling. In a discussion about intimacy in an interview for *The White Review* you note: "I am always dreaming of the ideal fiction." Can you elaborate here?

Diane Williams : The ideal fiction should deliver us from our isolation, provide comfort and new perspective – transport us with its new and enlivening music. It must accomplish much more than I can say.

Just too much. Too much.

While at work, I am blotting out a stack of words, moving others about – my goal being to write a sentence that can provoke a frisson that will lift me from my stupor and give me the courage to continue.

But the title I choose provides the first opportunity to stir myself up. "Jerry" once served as the title for my story-in-progress. He's an overbearing man and the name *Jerry*, for me, is numinous for reasons I cannot disclose. Except that yesterday I expunged this character altogether.

The current title is 'Given With Pleasure and Received with Admiration,' which was inspired by a picture book that features rings through the ages.

This title is also a prayer for the wished-for, happy collaboration between an author and a reader – a relation that ought to be key. Perhaps this title has the necessary scope and equilibrium to hold sway.

BSF : In your story "Beauty, Love and Vanity Itself" you write: "More needs to be said. Let me tell you where all eyes and minds are for the moment on the surface." – which could be a theme for a lot of your stories, and certainly a guide-post for how to write flash fiction: see what's on the surface, ponder what's beneath. How do you see the relationship between what's apparent and what's more hidden, and how does flash in particular work to reveal both, in your view?

DW : Well, in my view, there cannot be a standard formula that leads to a conception that one hopes will be unprecedented.

And here I must acknowledge that I am hostile to any label or category, such as "flash," that might unreasonably tag short, short stories as a fashion trend that necessitates a new name – a fashion trend that then predictably gutters out, as all fashions must do – for short, short stories have been in the world for millenniums.

Let me say, though, that the line from my story "More needs to be said" that you've quoted is especially haunting in this context – and this is because of my unwelcome conviction that "More **does not** need to be said."

Why struggle at this task when my literary heroes have already done the job brilliantly?

But how else to live?

I identify with Sherwood Anderson who said: "...what I wanted for myself most of all...was to try to develop, to the top of my bent, my own capacity to feel, see, taste, smell, hear."

About the Guest Editor

Aimee Bender is the author of five books—including *The Girl in the Flammable Skirt*, a NY Times Notable Book of 1998, international bestseller *The Particular Sadness of Lemon Cake*, and most recently *The Color Master*, which was a NY Times Notable Book of 2013. Her work has been published in *Granta*, *GQ*, *The Paris Review*, *McSweeney's*, *Tin House*, and more, as well as heard on "This American Life" and "Selected Shorts." She has been translated into sixteen languages. When in graduate school at University of California Irvine, she often turned in two stories because she was so interested in the shorter form (and at that point didn't write much that was longer); this turned out to be invaluable, because it allowed the workshop to point her towards the better work, which was not always obvious. Her first published short short, "The Rememberer," was printed in *The Missouri Review*, a journal she had tried for years and years. She teaches creative writing at University of Southern California, and lives in Los Angeles with her family.

CPSIA information can be obtained
at www.ICGtesting.com
Printed in the USA
FSHW011734240119
54864FS

9 780998 966779